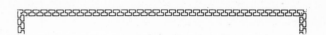

CONSTANT FIRE BY MELISSA HARDY

Parts of this book have appeared in *The New Quarterly* and *Exile*. I would like to thank Mary Ulmer Chiltoskey for providing me with excellent background material, the late Ollie Jumper for telling me about the rabbits, my mother Martha Nell Hardy for knowing a good story when she heard it and passing it on, with details, and my father William Hardy for what he thought was only the loan of nineteenth-century ethnologist James Mooney's invaluable *Myths of the Cherokee* and *Sacred Formulas of the Cherokees*.

This book was written and published with the assistance of the Canada Council, the Ontario Arts Council and others. Edited with the assistance of the Ontario Publishing Centre of the Ministry of Culture and Communications.

ISBN 0 88750 997 5 (hardcover)
ISBN 0 88750 998 3 (softcover)

Cover art by Ghitta Caiserman-Roth
Book design by Michael Macklem
Edited by David Helwig

Printed in Canada

PUBLISHED IN CANADA BY OBERON PRESS

This book is dedicated to the Eastern Band of the Cherokee.

Introduction

I had my first vision at the age of eight. It was also my last. I was skip-roping up a flight of cement stairs when I tripped. Possibly I passed out. What I remember, however, was not blackness but a slow, cinematic fade to centre which left the field of my vision a uniform, pulsating white. This fade was accompanied by an audio fade. Ambient sound—birdsong, the drone of insects, the catarrhal grind of a car pulling around the curve of the laneway—was gradually replaced by a silvery vibration that hummed just this side of sound. I had squeezed through an opening between worlds.

This alternate state of consciousness lasted just long enough for the child me to appraise the situation: it can be this way too, I remember thinking. Then, beginning at the centre of my vision and moving toward the periphery, a more familiar world began to reconstruct itself—the cement stairs that led from my neighbour's patio to her carport (Mrs. List, everything she owned was a silver blue, including her Christmas tree) the forest, or gulch as we called it, a sky that threatened rain.

It did rain that day and thunder mightily, and I was taken to the Catholic hospital across the river to have my nose X-rayed by nuns whose old-fashioned habits, my father told me, concealed the wheels that replaced their feet—these, apparently, had been lopped off at the ankle at the same time as their heads had been shorn. The holy two-wheelers pronounced my nose cracked. That fissure was a small price to pay for the foundation of understanding, for never again was I to confuse the apparent with the real.

I was fourteen the summer of 1966 when my parents joined the company of "Unto These Hills," the outdoor pageant, or, as the genre was called in its fifties' heyday, the symphonic drama re-enacting the events leading up to the removal of the

Cherokee people from their homeland to "Indian territory" beyond the Mississippi—the Removal is referred to as getsikahvda anegvi, which means The Trail On Which We Cried or the Trail of Tears.

The Cherokee once held the entire Allegheny region from the interlocking head-streams of the Kanawha and the Tennessee, extending southward almost to the site of Atlanta, and from the Blue Ridge Mountains on the east to the Cumberland range on the west. Their territory comprised an area of about 40,000 square miles and included parts of present-day Virginia, Tennessee, North Carolina, South Carolina, Georgia and Alabama.

The name by which they called themselves, Yunwiya, meant "The Principal People," (the word Cherokee seems rooted in a language other than their own, perhaps Choctaw) and a study of their language has revealed them to be of Iroquoian stock. How long they had resided in Cherokee country at the time they first encountered the white man is a mystery. They had a predilection for new gods, as their later, ready embrace of Christianity was to prove, and so their ritual forms and national epics had fallen into decay before the American Revolution, leaving behind only a fragmented migration myth to account for their wanderings on the planet.

More than any other tribe of Native Americans, the Cherokee embraced the ways of the white man. They inter-married freely, sent their children to be educated in Mission Schools, adopted white methods of husbandry and adapted their form of government to reflect the American model. By the early eighteen-hundreds, their chiefs were men of mixed blood, wealthy in land and slaves. They dwelt in plantation houses the green lawns of which were graced by flocks of strutting peacocks, and sent their sons north to prep schools where they learned to write sonnets by the book and surreptitiously courted young white ladies. Indeed, the town of Cornwall, Connecticut was so scandalized when two representatives of the flower of its maidenhood ran off with Cherokee youths that the citizens of the town forced the closure of the mission school where the couples had met.

The Cherokee adopted the ways of their white neighbours because they saw them as preferable to the old ways. They assumed that, in doing so, they safeguarded their right to remain on the land that had been theirs since before memory. They were, of course, very much mistaken.

To the Americans' way of thinking, Native Americans, no matter how civilized they might be, were still Indians and their destiny lay elsewhere than the land of their ancestors. Accordingly, in 1838, after a protracted struggle, President Andrew Jackson ordered that the Cherokee be rounded up and sent out west, beyond the Mississippi River, to Indian Territory in Oklahoma. Many eluded the soldiers sent to fetch them and hid out, landless fugitives, in the mountains of North Carolina, Tennessee and North Georgia. They, together with those who would later make the long journey back from Oklahoma on foot, became the ancestors of the modern-day Eastern Band of the Cherokee, the Cherokee I knew. (A great Cherokee sculptor, who descends from those who came back from Oklahoma, is named Going Back Chitolsky). Those who did not hide were marched out west under appalling conditions.

It is impossible to give the exact death toll of the Trail of Tears, but it may have been as high as 4000 people, a quarter of the immigrants. As the Holocaust forms a central event in the history of the Jewish people, a peg on which they hang their racial consciousness, so the Trail of Tears is the central event in the history of the Cherokee. Everything that came before was prologue; everything after, epilogue.

"Unto These Hills" chronicles the history culminating in this central event. The production, which opened in 1950 and is still going strong, boasts a cast and crew of well over a hundred people and plays to big houses in the Mountainside Theatre, an amphitheatre seating 3000 people. It is a hackneyed and dated vehicle, necessarily simplistic in its portrayal of a complicated series of events taking place over many decades, but it has become for many Cherokee their vision of their past, as was borne out by a controversy that took place about ten years ago over the choreography of one of the show's set pieces, the ancient Eagle Dance.

Back in the early fifties, a former dancer with Ted Shawn and Ruth St. Denis choreographed the Eagle Dance. Needless to say, Martha Graham's influence was unmistakeable. Many years later, a new choreographer researched the Eagle Dance and altered the choreography so that the dance in the show would be more historically accurate. The local Cherokee were furious. Their sacred Eagle Dance, the dance they had seen night after night since the show began so many years before, had been tampered with, violated. My father, by this time the show's Director, supported the choreographer for a while, then backed down, and the old Grahamesque Eagle Dance was reinstated to the considerable satisfaction of traditionalists.

"Unto These Hills" is one of the longest-playing and wealthiest outdoor dramas in the world. It owes its success in large measure to its location. Cherokee, the town where it takes place, is adjacent to the Smoky Mountain National Park. Thousands upon thousands of tourists pass through the park every year and, as bears are extremely hard to see at night, a large number of those tourists end up paying good money to be entertained by a recreation of their forefathers' brutality to Native Americans.

Like the recreated Oconaluftee Indian Village, a kind of native Williamsburg, and the Cherokee Historical Museum, "Unto These Hills" is a business venture of the Cherokee Historical Association. The show is tribally owned and run and is a major employer of local Cherokee. The cast includes about 50 Cherokee; numerous other natives are employed in the concession stands, as ushers and parking-lot attendants.

This is how I came first to know the Cherokee, backstage with all the other "Indian maidens." Every night we pulled on wigs of stiff black horsehair and painted each other from hairline to pantyline with a wet, terracotta-coloured slime called Texas Dirt to perform the Cherokee's most significant ritual, the Green Corn Dance. We then fled to the shower to wash our body paint off and repaint our faces so that we could reappear, clad this time in gingham dresses and poke bonnets, to be defrauded of our nation's patrimony. I was in the choir that sang "Amazing Grace" translated into Cherokee behind the flat of the stage church. This demonstrated the Cherokee's willing embrace of Christianity—very important if our drama's message was to impact in the Bible Belt. Finally, in Scene 12, before thousands of Americans munching popcorn, we began the long journey from these mountains, from our sacred homeland into a spotlight covered with yellow gel. We exited stage right toward a distant and strange land beyond the Father of Waters. We went west, a direction that the Cherokee have always associated with Death. The Darkening Land, the land of ghosts, lies to the west. Fittingly it is a journey on which 4000 of my fictive tribespeople would perish.

Night after night for seven years I went through the stylized motions of a history not my own, together with so many others down the years that now, when I return to Cherokee and sit in the audience to see the show, it is as if I am sitting in an echo chamber reverberating with all the voices and inflections of a generation of actors whom I have heard repeat those familiar lines. Night after night, I recreated the central event of the Cherokee nation. (I sweated Texas dirt well into my twenties, years after I left the show.) And by day, I moved among the remnant—those who had stayed behind; those who had come back.

Like those madcap girls of Cornwall, Connecticut, Sarah and Harriet, who married John Ridge and Elias Boudinot, I fell in love with Cherokee boys and kissed them backstage on the roof of the prop deck; I attended backwoods birthday parties that took place deep in the mountains, up dirt fireroads, over creeks that had to be crossed on frayed hemp bridges, in chinked and notched cabins like that of the Light-

Up-the-Skies; I came to the old women to learn what a woman needs to know, white or red: tatting and witching; how nature might be cajoled so that spells are cast and curses laid; that, to be a good conjure woman, you must be patient. The best curses, like cancer, work over time. Perhaps most importantly, these old women reinforced my understanding that the apparent is just a sub-category of the real. They taught me not to prioritize external stimuli as rigidly as whites tend to do, so that, when it might be good to do so, I could experience the life in everything more fully. I learned that there is a hunger on the part of what has died to walk once more with the living, that trees have spirits and fragments of human souls hang torn from their branches, that these souls fly through the forests like panicked birds before a fire.

Not only are the Eastern Cherokee different from white people, they are different from the Western Cherokee and, indeed, other native Americans. I cannot presume to define their culture—like all cultures, it is complex and beyond even the understanding of outsiders. Just a few, random observations:

Unlike most white men, the Cherokee utter profundities without a shred of self-consciousness. They also don't mince words about anyone they don't like. As a people they have for so long had so little to lose, that they wear their grudges very nonchalantly. They also love metaphor, particularly natural ones, and their speech fairly bristles with these. One of my favorites, uttered with apparent sincerity (although you can never be completely sure), was ,"As the crow flies, so does his shit fall!"

The Cherokee tend to take a dimly ironic view of things. They are a deeply humorous people but theirs tends to be an underdog humour, dark and fatalistic and played, for the most part, extremely deadpan. They are fond of jokes which have as their fulcrum the white man's stereotyped perception of Native Americans. For example, my grandfather, a Texas panhandler who spent most of his adult life on the Cherokee strip in Oklahoma, once had dinner with a member of the Western band, who was, incidentally, an educated man. They were served stew. When Granddaddy asked for a second helping, his Cherokee host handed him a longhandled wooden spoon. "Dig deep, white man," he said. "Puppy at bottom of pot."

Cherokee stories are not like the stories of white men, which end with warning. Cherokee stories break up like fights or modulate like music into a different key or drift away like smoke. The woman on whose funeral the funeral of Ivy Light-Up-the-Sky is based once told me a story: "When I was a little girl, I got sick," she told me. "Nobody knew what was wrong with me, not even the white doctor. Everybody said I would die. I was sick a long time. A whole winter I lay in bed. Only my mother believed that I would not die. She made me drink a kind of tea that she had made. It was very bitter. It was made out of rabbit tobacco. This is a kind of herb. It is also called Life Everlasting. One day my mother told me to get out of bed and come to the window. I got out of bed and came to her by the window and looked out into the forest. There were rabbits as far as I could see, rabbits everywhere. They were watching the house. They were watching the window. 'They have come to see you,' my mother told me. 'To see if you are well yet.' That day I did not go back to bed. Or the next day. Or the next."

I can make these generalizations and feel that they have some truth, but the Cherokee hold themselves in considerable reserve. Their hearts are tucked very far up their sleeves, where no white man will ever see them. Hence I have never seen what I was not intended to or understood more than was my lot. Some things, the Cherokee feel, are properly Cherokee. My mother tells a story. She was picking her way barefoot across a parking lot up on the compound where the cast and crew lived one day when she was stopped by one of the local Cherokee matriarchs, who happened to be driving by. "Martha Nell," the woman said,"what are you doing? Hasn't anybody told you that white women don't go barefoot outdoors?"

A more chilling application of this sense of propriety was a story that circulated about our resident medicine man. It is an origin myth, the story of how all the old women in the cast came to tat lace.

Once long ago a white travelling salesman seduced the medicine man's daughter. The medicine man didn't cotton to this, so he locked the salesman up in the sweatbox up at the Oconaluftee Indian Village. It was winter, and the village was closed for the season. Needless to say, the salesman died. The corpse was found in the spring. Everyone knew that the medicine man had done it. He had motive and a couple of other crimes to his name—he was widely suspected of having murdered a couple of people over in Tennessee with mismixed elixirs—true, he was not a very good medicine man, but these poisonings were believed to be deliberate. The case was complicated, however, by the medicine man's aged mother, who confessed to the salesman's murder and stuck to her story. She was convicted, but, because the judge knew she hadn't done it, given a light sentence. She learned how to tat in prison and, upon her return to the Boundary, taught the art to her friends. Old women have been tatting and selling their wares—they maintain to anyone who asks that this is a traditional mountain craft—by the highway ever since.

I left Cherokee for Canada and graduate school in history when I was 21. Thereafter I only visited the Qualla Boundary once a year. My family, however, have remained with the show these last 27 years, and my brother, who has come and gone over the years, but mostly come, has directed "Unto These Hills" for several years now.

Somehow I never wrote about the Cherokee. This was not because I was chary of appropriating their voice. The only option available to writers who don't appropriate voices is the production of more or less artfully veiled autobiographies. Autobiographies are not fiction. Fiction is fiction...things that haven't happened...make believe...elaborate lies that go on for page after page.

No, the reason I did not write about the Cherokee for so long is that I was reverent...which is another word for scared.

After all, Custer got his, and very deservedly too, for trying to open up the Black Hills to waggon trains and prospectors—the Black Hills were sacred to the Sioux. I always knew that, if I should choose to write about the Cherokee, given my family's close and long association with the tribe, I would be taking on a sacred trust. Sacred trusts are tricky items.

My immediate reason for finally breaking down and setting a story on the Boundary was an overpowering desire for vengence. To put it succinctly, I needed to ritually murder someone in the worst way. So I wrote "Magical Thinking," which appeared in *The New Quarterly* in 1990. In this story a half-breed woman returns to the Qualla Boundary and arranges for her grandmother, a conjure woman, to lay a curse on her former lover.

I had opened a door, and, beyond that door, lay a garden of thorny possibilities.

MELISSA HARDY

Blood

The Cherokee police—that's Ira Bushytail and Ollie Rattler—found Bob Pricey in the Spring. Dewayne Jumper, who manages the Oconaluftee Indian Village up by the Mountainside Theatre, gave them a call. "Smells pretty high up here in the Village," he told them. He was just opening up after the winter. "Something big's died, and that's for sure."

"You go poke around," they told him. They were busy taking a grain of liquor. "Call us if you find anything."

But Dewayne wasn't buying any. "You poke around," he told them tartly. "You're the goddam police."

14

Now, the Oconaluftee Indian Village is one of those recreated villages—folks call it the Redman's Williamsburg. It's got a square ground and places where the local people show the tourists how they did stuff in the old days: putting live coals into logs to make dugout canoes, or finger weaving belts, or carving fish hooks out of bone. And there's mud huts like the people used to live in long ago, and a seven-sided council house—one side for each of the seven clans—and it has one of those authentic sweatboxes they used to cure people or to torture them, a kind of dugout just high enough for a man to sit down in. They'd heat up a couple of big river rocks and pour some herb tea on them, and that'd make the vapour. Well, that's where they found Bob, locked up in that sweatbox. And he weren't looking his best neither. Been dead a long time.

Juanita Tuskateeskee sat singing on her front porch down in Deep Cove. Singing and rocking; rocking and tatting; shuttle and thread and an old, raggedy voice stringing knots and notes. She's old. Maybe a hundred years old. Nobody knows. Nobody wrote down what day she was born up there on Blood Mountain, and she's been around longer than anybody else on the Qualla Boundary. You ask anybody.

"Who caught his blood-o? Who caught his blood-o? 'I,' said the fish, 'with my little silver dish, it was I, O, it was I.'"

She warbles the next verse of the old ballad in a voice that sounds like a rusty blade dragged over a razor strop. Her feet don't quite reach the floor, though once they did: she's all shrivelled up like a raisin; she's the woman she was half a century before, only puckered up into a crone.

There's a white man sitting up on the porch with her, name of Don; he's a teacher from the college over at Culhowee that's making one of those song collections. Got a tape recorder purring away in his lap like a black cat. Says the way Juanita sings is Elizabethan; Elizabeth's one of those English queens who lived a ways back. Well, things don't change much in these parts, century to century, and that's a fact.

And just as she's singing, "Who sewed his shroud-o? Who sewed his shroud-o? 'I,' said the eagle, 'with my little thread and needle, It was I, O, it was I,'" the Cherokee police squad car comes bouncing up that old fire-trail. And it stops and out climb Ira Bushytail and Ollie Rattler. What with all the liquor they'd taken on and that old road that'll bounce the transmission out of a car and the guts out of a man, and the fact that what was left of Bob Pricey weren't too wholesome, they're feeling sort of piqued. "Where the hell's that grandson of yourn? Where the Hell's Coming Back?" Ira wants to know.

Coming Back Tuskateeskee was down Big Cove way up by Raven's Fork hunting the what-all he needs for this spell he's fixing to cast on his granddaughter Donella to fix her affections. Stalking plants like they was animals. Drawing nigh them from the South, where the White Woman that is love dwells, he steals up on mistletoe and trillium root and love-all-in-a-tangle like a thief.

As for Juanita who was Coming Back's grandmother, she took one look at Ollie and Ira and turned to Don and said, "You get you round back for a piece while I'm conversing with these boys." And he's polite, knows which side his bread is buttered on; so he heads on back to that tangledy clump of laurel folks call a bald and hunkers down and waits.

"What's going on?" Juanita asks, once he's out of earshot.

Bob Pricey came from somewhere down in Georgia, 'round Macon way, and what he was, while he was alive, was a running sore on two legs. Not a scrap of flesh about him, and he wore naugahyde trousers and a vest with fringe and a beat-up old hat with a frayed red feather in it—like he was an Indian, only he wasn't. He was one of these what they call Wannabees; had no notion whatsoever that there's no future in being an Indian.

"That Bob Pricey guy that took up with Donella...," Ira told Juanita. Donella was Juanita's great great granddaughter.

"We just found him in the Indian Village," said Ollie.

"Dead," said Ira.

Bob worked at the Dairy Queen down on the Oconaluftee River where it bends, hauling the formula in from Slyva City in that old semi of his, and that was where Donella worked too, at the Soft Serve machine. She was as soft and pretty as a lady dog's eyes, and he started sniffing around her, and she started sniffing around him. And seeing how love isn't much fancier than availability beset by opportunity, they fell in love.

"Yu! Ha!" Coming Back's down by the river's edge. "Now the souls have met, never to part, O Ancient One above," he cries softly in the Cherokee. He is spare and bent and his long white hair hangs loose to his shoulders. "O Black Spider," he chants, "you have let down your web." Coming Back circles a red trillium four times going from right to left. He sneaks about it in hightop sneakers a size too big; grimaces as he bends down and tugs the trillium up by its root (bending hurts his back; he's got rheumatism, what Cherokee call The Crippler). He drops a red bead into the hole, payment to the earth, then covers the hole with loose earth. "Her soul you have wrapped up with your web," he says softly, rising and turning to wind cobweb onto a forked stick.

"Somebody locked him in the sweathouse, Juanita," Ira continued. "Must have starved to death. Been there all winter, we reckon."

"Wonders to who that might have been," said Juanita, knowing.

One day Bob Pricey just didn't show up for work. That was back in October. He never did come back. Donella, she took on. Well, she was pregnant by that time. But the manager of the DQ, he figured Bob didn't cotton to the idea of a baby, just drifted down the road a piece. He was the kind would do that. So nobody went looking for him. Just let it slide slow like a snake downstream.

"Can't get the body out without taking off the top of the sweathouse," Ollie told Juanita. This had been a worry to him all the way up the mountain; he'd helped build that sweathouse when he was a kid with the Cherokee Boys' Club, and he felt kind of personal about it. "We tried pulling on him," he explained, "but he just come apart."

"His arm," explained Ira. "Come off at the joint like he was a cooked turkey."

"He's cooked all right," agreed Ollie.

"The thing is, the FBI's got to know about this," Ira told her. The Boundary, being an Indian reservation, is federal land. "And the first thing they're going to do, you bet you, they're going to come looking for Coming Back."

They were all quiet then, thinking as how it was true; out back Don had stood to piss into the laurel bald. He thought they couldn't hear, but they were Indians, after all.

Now Coming Back that was Juanita's grandson and Donella's granddaddy had him two jobs, one for the summertime and one for the wintertime. In the summer what he did was he sat out in front of this sort of paper mâché only it was plasticized teepee in downtown Cherokee, wearing this Plains Indian outfit he'd lifted from one of those costume rental places down in Atlanta—buckskins and one of those big headdresses with all the feathers—never mind that there never was a Cherokee Indian wore such gear—with a sign that read "Get Your Picture With the Chief!" and those tourists would come along and have their polaroid pictures taken with him and give him five dollars apiece for the loan of his red face.

As Ollie and Ira drove off, Juanita's muttering to herself in Cherokee up on that porch. "Sge! Ka'lanu U'nage...." She's calling down the Black Raven, thinking how she might as well be with her now that people were looking for other people. Meanwhile, that Don teacher man comes creeping around the house, calling, "Is it okay now, Juanita? Can I come back?"

"Oh!" and "Sure," she says, and she starts up singing, "Who made the coffin? Who made the coffin? 'I,' said the snipe, 'with my little pocket knife, it was I, O, it was I.'"

Come winter, Coming Back ran security on the Indian Village, on account of he lived hard by, up Mt. Noble. And he did the rounds every six hours or so, riding a Colt 45 in his hip pocket. If Bob Pricey had screamed, if he had yelled, "Let me out!" or, "Help! Help!" Coming Back would have heard. And Bob must have yelled. In the beginning he must have yelled and yelled, there on his hands and knees like a dog, but there was nobody to hear him in the winter with the tourists gone and the place locked up. Nobody but Coming Back Tuskateeskee, who made the rounds; who lived up that way; who had the only key to the village gate.

Juanita started into the next verse. "Who lowered him down-o? Who lowered him down-o? 'I,' said the crane, 'with my little golden chain, it was I, O, it was I.'" Then she stops her rocking all of a sudden, and she's staring ahead of her at the world of shape and shadow beyond the porch rail—cataracts laid over her black eye pupils like pectin over jam. She doses herself for them—the juice of a gill-go-by-the-grounds mixed with a little honey—but they're too thick now for shifting, and, if you tell her she can get them burnt off her down at the hospital over there in Asheville, she'll tell you this: "I've seen it all. Why the goddamned hell would I want to see it again?" This is what she sees in the black eye of her mind:

The black raven comes. She has been called. Coming Back has called her. She comes from the West where death abides. She circles the sweatbox built by Ollie Rattler and the Cherokee Boys' Club. It is a night in late October; the moon rises full, lighting up the Ceremonial Ground with its cold light. To the west of the ground, Coming Back and Bob Pricey sit, crouched down, huddled in the sweatbox, dragging on a bottle of corn whisky, having a smoke. The Black Raven flies high but sees all, hears all. Her eyes are telescopes; her ears, microphones. Being a raven, she sees and hears as a raven does.

She sees Bob Pricey's soul glitter in the dark like a scrap of tin; she hears his voice as a series of coos, low and contented. Bob Pricey is happy, happy to be drinking with Coming Back, a real Indian; he feels accepted, one of the tribe at last. And so he should, he thinks, seeing as to how he had taken up with Donella, how she is going to bear his child. They are connected by blood now, him and Coming Back. The blood binds them. The Raven can hear no fear in Bob Pricey's voice and knows that he is a fool, to sit with his great enemy Coming Back and to suspect nothing.

But Don is fidgeting. "Well?" he says at last.

"Well, what?" Juanita asks.

"You've stopped singing," he says.

"That was the last verse," Juanita tells him tartly, closing her eyes.

This is what the Black Raven sees:

Inside the sweatbox it is cold and dark and smells of earth and earthworms. The two men drink Coming Back's whisky. With their cigarettes they burn red holes into the coarse, grainy darkness. Though the old man keeps to himself, is stiff, gruff, the young man, warmed by the whiskey, by the old man's presence, becomes expansive, swells to fill the place. He talks much about little. Finally the old man, disgusted, shuffles to his feet. "Got to piss," he tells Bob Pricey. And out he goes.

Bob Pricey, he's drunk now; he feels good; the old man, her grandfather, takes him drinking, shares whisky with him, accepts him. No-one has ever accepted Bob Pricey before. Not his father who blew Macon before he was old enough to put a face to the name of 'Daddy', not his mother that worked at Woolco in candy and a-sooned he'd never been born, he was such a burden to her. All his life everybody yelling at him like he was some dog in the middle of the road wouldn't move even if you honked and honked. Just maybe he was a little slow, that was all. Out of time. Like an Indian. But being an Indian was something. Noble. Ancient. Hell, thought Bob Pricey. I run deep. I do. And he had tied into it: the oldness, the being right with God and time; bought blood with seed.

Now most people in these mountains, they married and mixed. They'd marry anything but one of those Negroes. (Nothing a Cherokee cottons to less than a Negro; to them the Negroes are the despised of this earth, and Negroes know it and stay away.) So, 'cause of all this marrying and mixing with white folks, some of those who call themselves Cherokee are as white as the blooming on a dogberry; they got no more than maybe two or three drops of Indian blood in their veins.

But the Tuskateeskees and those others up Blood Mountain way.... They left the white folks alone by and large. Weren't a quadroon among 'em; naught less than a half breed. And you have to say that nobody thought much about it one way or the other; it was just the way things fell out; but later, when the people started talking Red Power down in Cherokee, those Tuskateeskees got right up about their bloodedness. They got blood proud's what they did. "Ain't nothing white about my family," Juanita used to say.

Which is why things fell out the way they did.

This is what the Black Raven sees when she closes her eyes:

Bob lies back against the mouldery grass that pads the bunks in the sweatbox and listens to the wind in the trees and the high-pitched silver whine of the moon and to Coming Back's pee sizzle dark against the cold rock. Then, nearer to his ears, he hears the sound of the sweathouse door shutting, of the bolt being drawn.

"Hey, Coming Back?" Bob objects, and he rises onto one elbow. "Hey, man!" He laughs nervously. "What's going on?"

But Coming Back doesn't answer. It's a kind of torture, not answering.

"Hey, man," calls Bob, and he tries to stand up. It's hard, because the ceiling's so low. "Hey, man, this ain't funny." Coming Back disagrees. Standing a few yards off, he begins the spell. He speaks in a low voice. He sounds like the wind.

"Listen!" he says. "Now I have come to step over your soul. Your soul I have put at rest under the earth." With a stick he scrapes a bit of Bob's spittle from the mouth of the whisky bottle and pokes it down into a joint of wild parsnip.

"Coming Back!" cried Bob, his voice full of fear. "Don't kid around. Don't fuck with me, man!"

"I have come to cover you over with a black rock," murmured Coming Back. "I have come to cover you over with the black cloth. I have come to cover you with the black slabs, never to reappear." He thrust into the parsnip tube a paste of earthworms, splinters from a tree struck by lightning.

Bob rattled the door until the hinges creaked. He moaned.

"Toward the black coffin of the upland in the Darkening Land your paths shall stretch out," said Coming Back. Hunkering down, he dug a hole with a stick at the base of a tree. "So shall it be for you. The clay of the upland has come to cover you. Instantly the black clay has lodged there where it is at rest at the black houses in the Darkening Land." He placed the tube in the ground and laid seven yellow stones on top of it to secure it.

"Oh, Coming Back," moaned Bob. "Let me out! Coming Back? Where are you? Are you there?"

"Now your soul has faded away," Coming Back told him softly. "It has become blue. When darkness comes, your spirit shall grow less and dwindle away, never to reappear. Listen!" He stood with difficulty. It was damp. His rheumatism was acting up. Then he shoved the key to the sweatbox into his pocket and walked slowly off. The shuffle of his shoes through the wood chips on the path made a sound like gobbets of earth falling on the lid of a coffin.

"Hey, man!" screams Bob Pricey. "Hey, man! I don't understand!"

"He is yours," Coming Back told the Black Raven. Then he left the village, taking care to lock the gate behind him.

And the Black Raven was happy, for she had longed for the glittering scrap of soul, and so she circled downwards.

As for Donella, well, this is what Coming Back did for her: cooked her up a mess of wormwood, elecompane, tamarack and the snuff off a devil's snuffbox in spirits of turpentine , and after it was as thick and dark as a hog's liver, he put it in the ashes of a fire and let it set there for a spell of two days, blood warm under a waning moon. He'd killed worms that way and a couple of folks down in Eastern Tennessee. Donella was sick for a spell, then she lost that half-breed baby of hers.

"Who killed Cock Robin? Who killed Cock Robin...?"

Juanita's singing to herself this time, lost in the wash of a hundred years; she likes those old songs; she rides them like they was horses taking her to a far place. The puncheon floor, cut from a yellow poplar, creaks as she rocks, producing a strain that is its own harmony.

"Who killed Cock Robin? Who killed Cock Robin? 'I,'" said Donella. "With my hair and my eyes, it was I, O, it was I."

"Who sewed his shroud-o? Who sewed his shroud-o? 'I,'" said Juanita. "With my shuttle and my thread, it was I, O, it was I."

"Who made the coffin? Who made the coffin? 'I,'" said Ollie Rattler. "With the Cherokee Boys' Club, it was I, O, it was I."

"Who lowered him down-o? Who lowered him down-o? 'I,'" said Coming Back. "With my gun and my key and a bottle of whisky, saying, 'Come on up to the village, Bob; keep me some company. I'll tell you how it feels to be an Indian, alone, in a dark place and hungry, and we'll have us a long, long drink.' It was I, O, it was I."

"We Tuskateeskees was ever a mystery to the white man," says Juanita. She's speaking on the inside of her head now. She's speaking to the white men who will come, asking for her grandson; to all the white men she's ever known in all her many—God knows how many they are too—years; to all the white men any Indian has ever met up with since the first day they came upon one another in these valleys, and the white man said to the Indian, "This land is mine," and the Indian said, "I see things different." "Our red faces are like stone walls," says Juanita now. "A white man couldn't get to the place behind our eyes to save his life. And, iffen he could, he'd be et up. Et up by the fire, by our memories that are like live coals—mine and my father's and my grandfather's before me. One thing you got to cotton about the Tuskateeskees; we'uns mean. Cut you as soon as look at you. Shred you like wheat. My granddaddy it was walked the Trail of Tears and back again from the Oklahoma territory out west. Come back to join those that had stayed, that had hid out in these mountains. Twelve hundred miles of hard trail, and along it the bones of the Cherokee. It were a fire that forged him, that trail; he come out the other end a hard man. And that's why he was called what he was: Coming Back. And the name came down with the blood, down the generations. And the hardness, the iron, the hate. Which is why the blood's important. Why we keep it like we do."

Coming Back returned from the woods shortly after Don left.

Juanita told him about Ollie and Ira's visit. "You'd best get you back into the mountains," she counselled him. "Up near the council house of the Nunnehi. Ain't no white man going to go up them bear trails."

Coming Back nodded. He squinted up at the blue cloudless sky through the pine trees with his old eyes. "Good thing it's been a dry one so far," he told her. "Else my bones be contrary-ing me."

On his way to the Council House of the Nunnehi, Coming Back stops by the river and takes the trillium root and the sprig of mistletoe and the love-in-a-tangle. He wraps a stretch of cheesecloth around them and ties the package up with a bit of string. Then he throws it into the very centre of Big Cove, Saligugi, Turtle Place, where the monster turtle lives. He waits, hunkers down on the shore and watches. Across the river, on Highway 19, there is traffic: tourists down from Sugarlands, RVs and vans leaking the noise of white men like oil onto the road.

But the package is easy. It floats like a leaf. The enemy turtle does not rise and eat it. The water does not claim it. After ten minutes of watching it straddle the smooth back of the river, Coming Back takes a stick and hooks the package. He is satisfied. The earth is not angry; the charm will work. Donella will fall in love again, with a man of blood this time; her babies will be Cherokee.

Long Man the River

Shall we gather at the river,
Where bright angels' feet have trod,
With the crystal tide forever
Flowing past the throne of God?

Well! I'd have reckoned that to be one of those what you'd call moot questions, thought Liza Light-Up-The-Sky Talahawa, who was standing on the bank of the Oconaluftee at nine o'clock on a Sunday morning in late autumn, cracking her knuckles apprehensively in grim expectation of her imminent total immersion in the river's icy water. The dull, pewter-coloured mist that hugged the river like its ghost had not yet stirred and dissipated, but already the folks of Yellow Hill had collected on the shores of the Oconaluftee to do their churching. Preacher Josiah Etowah had chosen to meet down here near Birdtown where the river shallows out on its way to join the Tuckasegee near Ela instead of up in Yellow Hill on account of Peggie Whistle, the big-headed dwarf woman who stood with her armpits draped over a pair of Canadian crutches at Liza's side.

"I cannot undertake to drown any poor seeker after salvation in the ebullient and raging Blood of the Lamb," Josiah had explained to his parishioners. Well, the Oconaluftee up at Yellow Hill doesn't rage exactly, but it does run chin-high on a grown man.

> On the margin of the river,
> Walking up its silver spray,
> We will walk and worship ever,
> All the happy golden day.

Actually, it was more of what Liza would call a mizzling sort of day—just this side of rainy.

> Ere we reach the shining river,
> Lay we every burden down;
> Grace our spirits will deliver,
> And provide a robe and crown.

Liza glanced back over her shoulder at the throng of parishioners who sat huddled and hunch-shouldered on blankets spread over the bumpy, sparse grass. It's a moot question, seeing as how we're already gathered by the river, she thought. Then she cracked her knuckles once again, speculatively but also nervously, making a dry, pod-snapping kind of sound, like the report of a distant BB gun—Liza could be as annoying as she was fine looking, big-boned and lithe-tall in a rayon dress splashed with big rust-coloured leaves that hugged her figure like a lover.

> Soon we'll reach the shining river,
> Soon our pilgrimage will cease,
> Soon our happy hearts will quiver
> With the melody of peace.

Peggie, who enjoyed quite a reputation as a joker, decided to chat Liza up during the hymn-singing. "What did the Indian say to his neighbour after he watched Columbus get down from his ship?" she hissed.

"I don't know," said Liza, who hated jokes.

"There goes the neighbourhood!" Peggie retorted, hacking with dry laughter.

Liza snorted.

The congregation ploughed into the refrain:

> Yes, we'll gather at the river,
> The beautiful, the beautiful river,
> Gather with the saints at the river
> that flows by the throne of God.

"The only problem is that first it flows by the motels in downtown Cherokee," Peggie continued, wiping tears of laughter from her eyes with the back of one arm. "And the motels dump all the white man's sewage into it! Heh! Heh!"

Liza stood, staring at the river, remembering foaming water, littered with red and yellow and brown leaves.... It was just as it had been when her father had made her go to water for the first time. She searched the surface of the water for evidence of the creature that lived in these depths...for the broad streak of firefly green that betrayed its presence. Then suddenly she caught herself. This rite is important, she told herself. You must try and keep control of yourself. Try not to let the others know. In an effort both to reclaim and advertise her equilibrium, she feigned nonchalance: wrinkled up her fine, proud nose—it arched bonily like the back of a cat—and shook back her hair from her shoulders. Despite the fact that she was no girl, she still wore it long and black and loose to her waist.

Like the irreverent Peggie Whistle, Liza was here to be baptized, but not because she had seen anything resembling The Light. What she had seen was Walter Reginald Barkman, that white man who owned not only the Oconaluftee Joke and Rock Shop down at the juncture of Highway 441 and Highway 19, but the adjoining laundromat and a photo-finish kiosk across the way as well. He was in one of his available phases right now. Women were forever taking up with Wally Barkman, then leaving him—so much so that folks lost count.

Well, Liza was dirt sick of being poor. Her husband of ten years, Ronnie Talahawa, had died two years this December leaving her with nothing but 223 purely worthless baseball cards, an eviction notice and the selfsame handful of dreams she had walked down the aisle with a decade before...if you could call standing up in front of the Justice of the Peace of Swain County walking down the aisle. Died of an aggravated case of drinking sour mash. It was coming to him, all right; he'd been working on it for years, honing his self-destructive techniques to a pure perfection.

And those dreams she had brought to the marriage...they were all creased now and bent out of shape. However, all that would be set right again, once she had Wally Barkman firmly in tow. Lucky for her that she had not outgrown that gaunt, hybrid beauty—the high cheekbones and the bold nose and the big, strangely russet-coloured eyes fringed with dark lashes that had once made her the talk of the Boundary. It had come to her down through her father, Joe Light-Up-The-Sky, whose family was descended from the Old Settlers out in the Oklahoma territory and was the result of the high incidence of

29

intermarriage that had taken place in that no-man's-land nineteenth-century unakas, white men, called Indian Territory.

"Now, here's one," Peggie offered, breathless. "What was Custer wearing at his last stand?" Baited by the tall woman's dismissive attitude, Peggie could not resist the temptation to annoy her.

She was like a cat that way. When she had been younger and more mobile, she had made a practice of biting about the ankles those people who ignored her .

"I don't know," said Liza.

"An arrow shirt," Peggie erupted, cackling.

A gold Pontiac LeMans nosed into the shoulder of the road. Power brakes bit into the loose gravel, power windows rolled up, and Wally Barkman stepped out of the driver's seat onto the pavement. "Hi, Darlin'!" he waved. He held something...a cloth of some sort...draped over one arm. Not properly a member of this congregation of Cherokee Baptists, he came no farther but stayed where he was, up by the road—he leaned against the side of his big car and lit up a Camel cigarette.

Wally was fifteen years Liza's senior. He was bald, had a pink face spangled with golden freckles and a stomach that hung down so low that it covered his you know even when he stood. Every time he wanted to do something with that thing, he had to haul his big stomach out of the way. He had come down to see her baptized—well, it was all his idea and doing, after all. Wally was one of those Born Again Christians, prone to lapses, forever on a wild yo-yo between Salvation and Perdition, and right now he was on a redemptory swing.

Liza swore under her breath. Ka nu nu. Bullfrog. She was riled. She felt as if a wide-toothed comb were being dragged down her spinal cord. Oh, she knew full well why Wally was here. He didn't trust her to follow through with her promise to embrace Jesus Christ as her Saviour. He had come to make sure that she fulfilled her end of the bargain he had struck: you take Jesus Christ as your Saviour, darlin', and I'll take you as my wife. Her rejection of Christianity had always been a point of pride with her. Alone of all her family she had followed Joe Light-Up-The-Sky in hating the white man's religion. "One of the things unakas gave the Indian was Jesus Christ," Joe used to say. "The other thing that comes to mind is smallpox." Liza wanted to scream and tear her hair and her clothes and jump all around like the crazy woman that she was inside, but instead, she just lifted her hand and smiled gently in Wally's direction, as meek and mild as that fellow Jesus himself. In return, he lifted his pudgy hand in silent salute.

There is no territory so thoroughly negotiated as that dark boundary between a woman and a man about to bind themselves together for whatever measure of eternity will fall to their lot.

But now Preacher Josiah Etowah was shuffling toward Liza and Peggie in his big galoshes, passing a battered Bible from one hand to the other like it was a football. His rusty black preacher's coat flapped open in the slight breeze that blew up from the river to reveal a black diver's wetsuit. "You ready for the symbolic death and resurrection of your soul, Sister Liza?" he asked in a ringing, adenoidal voice that did not sound natural in a man of his bulk—it sounded as if it were generated by some electrical implant.

Liza glared combatively at him from under her fringe of lashes. "I reckon," she said.

"How about you, Sister Whistle?" Josiah turned to Peggie. He inclined toward her, big, untidy and stained.

"Is the Pope Catholic?" Peggie quipped, poking at the toe of his galoshes with the rubber-tipped end of one of her crutches. "No, seriously, reverend, I've put the bean bread out and the kettle on and I am ready to receive my Saviour with a heart full of joy and understanding," she assured him.

"Well, that's good...that warms my heart, Peggie," said Josiah. He turned to his congregation. "Brothers and sisters...hello, hello! Thank you for getting up this fine Sunday morning and coming all this way down to Birdtown to join us in the solemn baptizing of our sisters in Christ...I'm talking about Mrs. Liza Talahawa here and Miss Peggie Whistle...."

In the meantime, Peggie was yanking at Liza's sleeve. "Hey! Hey!" she insisted. "Listen a minute. Now, this is a good one. Why were the Indians the first ones on the continent?"

"This is no time for joking around," Liza admonished her.

"Oh, the Lord likes a good laugh as well as anyone!" Peggie argued. "Otherwise how could He face another morning, with the dog's lunch He's made of the world? Listen up now. The Indians were the first ones on the continent because...they had reservations!"

Liza thought back to the first time she had become acquainted with Long Man the River: it had been when she was only a few weeks old.

Her father Joe wished his firstborn to be intelligent and to have a fine memory, so he engaged the services of Coming Back Tuskateeskee, who was a conjure man. According to the ancient rite, Coming Back gathered burrs of the jimsonweed. Because burrs hold fast to any object they come in contact with, they have the power to improve memory. Coming Back beat the burs into a paste and mixed it with water taken from Mingo Falls, which is on the other side of Stoney Mountain Ridge. There were two reasons why he did this. The first is that a river seizes and holds fast anything that is cast upon its surface, as Joe wished Liza's mind to do. The second reason is that the noise of the cataract from which the water was taken is the voice of Yunwi Gunnahita, the river god. The water, therefore, contains within it lessons a child might absorb. He gave the mixture to Joe to feed Liza on four successive days.

After she had eaten Coming Back's mixture, Liza became very sick and almost died. Her mother, Ivy Light-Up-The-Sky, was fit to be tied. "That's it," she said. Her father had built the

Yellow Hill Baptist Church. She had no use for conjuring save on those occasions when she needed a proper curse—Christianity is woefully lacking in the curse department. She packed Joe a bag and put it outside the cabin door. That meant divorce in Cherokee. From that day on, Joe no longer lived with them, though he often came up to the cabin to set a while with Ivy and visit with the girlchild who was to be his only spawn.

As for Liza, it was as if she had imbibed the god's voice at top volume and now there was no way of getting inside to turn that volume down. In any case, she could not remember back to a time when she did not hear a roaring in her ear or the whisper of hushed voices. And she remembered...everything.

"Now, you know what the old song says?" Josiah Etowah reminded his congregation. "John the Baptist was a preacher.... Some folks said he was a Jew.... Some folks said he was a Christian.... But he was a Baptist too!"

The congregation obliged him with a refrain:

I'm going to walk that lonesome valley!
I'm going to walk it for myself!
Nobody else can walk it for me!
I'm going to walk it for myself!

Liza remembered that the first time she had actually gone to the water was when she was a little girl maybe eight years old. Now, going to the water is different from going down to the river. It's not a casual thing at all, and Cherokee have done it for as long as anyone can remember. Going to the water is a rite, like baptism in that it involves total immersion, but unlike baptism in that it is appropriate to many occasions—the rising of a new moon, for example, or the greening of the corn, or when a sickness is strong enough to call for strong medicine. During the several epidemics of smallpox that had afflicted the Cherokee in the past, sufferers had always gone to the water, with the result that many died—this was of course preferable to disfigurement. Going to water is not dependent on any change of outlook, but only upon a recognition of what is—Grandfather Fire, and the sun that the conjurors put up in the heavens because, before they did, it had been too dark to see, and water, always water. These are the things that are.

It was Liza's father Joe who took her to the water: big, handsome Joe with a profile off the backside of a nickel and the heavy shoulders and the big hands. He thought it might cure her of the whispering voices in her head, the constant roaring in her ears. It was late autumn at the time, as now, and, as now, leaves covered the surface of the river.

"This is good," Joe said, pressing the heels of his hands hard together as he always did and shifting his shoulders. He was forever shifting his shoulders...this way and that, as if their weight were a yoke too heavy for him to bear comfortably, as if he were trying to redistribute the weight somehow. "The leaves give their medicine to the water," he explained. "They make the medicine stronger."

Liza knelt and touched the water. "It's too cold, Pa," she objected.

"Cold is only a feeling," Joe told her, taking hold of her underneath her armpits and plunging her into water so deep that her feet did not touch bottom.

Liza came down with a chill, developed pneumonia, became delirious and for some time left her body, taking the shape of a raven. The period of her life spent as a raven she remembers in dreams. Upon her waking, these dry to a dust, which settles imperceptibly all about her but through which all light is filtered.

Later, after she had recovered from her illness, her father fell from the suspension bridge from the road to Saunooke's Village and drowned. His bloated, rock-battered body was found downriver, washed up in those shallows out back of the Drama Motel a couple of miles down Highway 441.

It is said that he was drunk, but Liza knew full well that he had been lured into the river by an uktena. She knew because Joe had told her all about the giant serpent, which is so dangerous that even looking at it might be enough to kill a person—he was, Joe had told her, always on the lookout for an uktena, and one day he would find one. Its body is as thick as the trunk of a tree, he explained, its scales glitter blue like ice in the moonlight, and on its antlered head shines a bright crystal, an ulunsuti. This crystal ensures its owner success in hunting, love, rainmaking, and, most especially, in fore-telling whether someone will live or die—Joe wished very much to own an ulunsuti , and he had reason to hope since there were men who had succeeded in wresting it from the forehead of an uktena, among them Hugh Hefner and Howard Hughes. On the other hand, many men have died trying to possess a ulunsuti—the bright light it gives off so befuddles a man's senses that he cannot help but rush toward it...and his own doom. Liza's father Joe Light-Up-The-Sky was numbered among these unfortunate victims of their own desire.

Unfortunately, going to the water had not cured Liza of the voices in her head or the rushing sound in her ears. And the loss of her father so cracked her heart that it became ever after a fragile thing, subject to breaks and leakage.

"Yes, John the Baptist...he was a Baptist too!" repeated Josiah, echoing the words of the song. "He was the first Baptist. And why was he was a Baptist?"

"Because he baptized!" cried the congregation.

"And where did he baptize?"

"He baptized in the river!"

"And who did he baptize in the river?" cried Josiah.

"He baptized the Lord Jesus Christ in the river!" the congregation hollered back.

"Amen!" Josiah praised the Lord.

"Amen!" the congregation followed suit.

Shortly after Joe died, Liza began having those spells of hers. Not all the time. Just some of the time. One minute Ivy'd be talking to her, and she'd be listening, then other sounds would start to creep in and gradually dominate her hearing—the crunching sound of a female praying mantis chewing off the head of its mate on the branch outside the window, the dull thud of soil dropped from a gravedigger's spade onto the lid of a coffin in a graveyard a quarter of a mile away, the wind in the trees and the sound a distant fire sings to the brush as it eats it.

Or objects would lose their absolute definition and either dissolve into a shimmer or become strangely fluent. Her mother's chair would buzz busily away like a hive of electro-magnetic particles. Floors would bubble and sway like quag-mires. Tables would heave and buck like the water in a waterbed when you jump on it. Actual water, on the other hand, became as thick and metallic in its texture as mercury. The sound droplets made hitting a hard surface was as loud and jarring as brass balls poured from a bucket onto the floor of a high-school gymnasium.

But what was even more overwhelming was that, when a spell was come upon her, she began to experience a life in everything. She could hear the groans of the grass as it strained to grow up through the soil. She could feel as a hard knot in her chest the alarm of a bear she could not see, which sensed her walking downwind of the cave in which her young were hidden. Most peculiar of all, the eggs in her body spoke with her familiarly and called her Mother.

Coming Back had taken her down to the water again, this time at Ivy's behest—she simply did not know what to do with the girl who would rise in the wee hours of the night and go reeling around the cabin like a drunk, trying to pinpoint in a vortex of shadow the location of mysterious glittering objects, which haunted her dreams. "Get back to bed, Liza!" her mother would holler—thin, shrill voice in the gloom. "There are eight people sleeping in this cabin! You're waking folks up!"

So the gaunt old man with the long, piss-yellow hair had rattled beads and noted the movement of fish and admonished his patient to concentrate, concentrate, but it is an altogether different matter to fix the attention of an infant and of someone who is no longer a child. It involves taboos that must be observed for up to seven days, and Liza at the moment was incapable of focus. Then, one afternoon in Spring, toward the end of her time with Coming Back, she started to her feet and pointed to the river.

"Sit down, Liza!" Coming Back ordered. His voice was weary. How this girl tried his worn-shiny patience!

"But it's an uktena!" Liza cried, pointing. "There! Below the surface!"

"Send the uktena to the river below the river," Coming Back instructed her—for there is a world below this, like ours in every respect, except that there the seasons are different. The streams that come down from the mountains are the trails to that world. "Send the uktena home," he said. He had had enough of this crazy teenage girl. He wanted the money and the two pullets Ivy had promised him and to be done with it. Crouching by a damp river for several hours the past few days had aggravated his rheumatism to the point where he felt as if he had been flayed and then nailed up inside the stiff exoskeleton of a crawdad with instructions to escape as best he could.

But Liza had run to the shore and stood poised on the bank, peering into the water at the lithe body that coiled and uncoiled as fluorescent as a jewel between the dark green water.

"Why did you take my father?" she cried.

The uktena did not answer but only swam deeper until all
that bespoke her presence was a green glow in the depth of the
river.

Liza stamped her foot and cried.

And from that time on, not only had Liza heard voices in her
head and a roaring in her ears...not only did she fall into fits,
but she also was quarrelsome. For it is a well known fact that
anyone who loses their temper when they are going to water
will be quarrelsome for the rest of their lives.

"Are you ready, Sister Talahawa?

"What?" Liza snapped.

"Are you ready for holy baptism?" It was Josiah Etowah,
inclining toward her.

"Oh.... I 'spose," said Liza ungraciously, apprehensively.
She glanced quickly toward the road at Wally Barkman. The
owner of the Oconaluftee Rock and Joke Shop still leaned
against the Pontiac with his arms folded across his chest and a
cigarette poking out of his mouth. He nodded by way of
acknowledging her glance and made a flicking motion with
the fingers of one hand as if to urge her forward. She turned
back to Josiah. "Let's get this over with," she said and took the
steadying hand he offered her.

Together preacher and convert negotiated the rocky
bottom of the river like dancers navigating a crowded ball-
room until they had reached its cold centre. Liza was numb,
white-lipped with cold and dread. She knew for a certainty
that the uktena was in the river. Why should she not be? She
lived in the river. She had always lived in the river. And Liza
was afraid of the uktena. So afraid. Peering downstream, she
thought she detected movement and a glimmer of light,
firebug green, below the water's leafstrewn surface. The blood
blew through her veins like a firestorm, and she tried to pull
her hand free of Josiah's.

"Come on, now," he said. "It's almost over," and, placing one hand firmly upon her head, he said, "Take a breath now," and shoved it underwater.

She saw the uktena then, saw her clearly, the powerful, languorous body draped in a loose coil about her feet, the irridescent sheen of her plated scales, the yellow headlamps of her eyes. The creature rubbed against her leg as seductively as a cat.

It seemed to her that Josiah was pulling on her, trying to get her to surface, but she ignored him.

Why did you kill Joe Light-Up-The-Sky? she demanded of the uktena, but in her head, not with words. Why did you kill my father?

This time the uktena replied, also not with words. She spoke on the inside of Liza's skull in a language of tones: I have no agenda apart from opportunity, the uktena assured her. Like any creature, I take what I can when it is offered me by the means I have at my disposal. In this I act no differently than you. But enough of that. Come. See this ulunsuti I wear in my forehead?

And, turning, she thrust the bulging crystal embedded in the cavity between her eyes toward Liza's face. It was as roughly faceted as a thing found in nature and gave off a glow that was more milky than bright.

Josiah yanked at her. She could hear him calling to her through the thickened water. "Mrs. Talahawa! Mrs. Talahawa!"

She tried to twist free from his grasp.

If you pluck this from me, you will have success in love and in hunting...in all matter of things, the uktena assured her. It is what your father wanted too.

Liza had just reached her hand out for it when Josiah reached underwater and, seizing her by the chin, dragged her face up into the air. Liza coughed and choked.

"What do you think you were doing? Why did you fight me? If you want to drown yourself, do it yourself!" he hissed angrily. With more force than was strictly necessary, he shoved her toward the shore. She stumbled on the slippery rocks and almost fell.

In the meantime, Peggie Whistle was scrambling crutch over crutch toward the road like a stifflegged quadruped, screaming, "Not me! I've changed my mind! Did you see? That preacher almost drowned her! No! No! Salvation is not worth dying for!"

Wally Barkman threw his cigarette down, ground it into the gravel, and, adjusting the object draped over his arm, started down the hill toward the bank of the river. When Liza stumbled ashore, spent and soaked and trembling, he stepped forward and spread the object wide. In this way, with a red, green and white striped Hudson's Bay blanket, he took possession of the Indian woman who, at the very moment of her baptism, had been engaged in conversation with a river monster that had a vested interest in her family.

After her baptism, Liza took a chill and for a time was very ill. When she recovered, she married Wally Barkman. However, she never did get rid of the voices whispering inside her head or the roaring in her ears and, when she woke into the darkness of her night, it was always with fingers spread and tense, straining to grasp the bright, elusive, powerful crystal lodged within the vortex of shadow. Ever after.

Bean Bread

Arminty Quail had her first stroke while she was out hunting
yellowjackets for soup. That was early one morning during
that sweet patch of blackberry winter we had back in...oh, '85
or thereabouts. What she had intended to do was to gather a
whole comb of yellowjackets—the ground-dwelling kind—
and set it over the fire. First right side up to loosen the uncovered grubs, then upside down to parch its paperlike cover (the
beatinest thing: insects making a thing so like paper to live
inside of, thought Arminty as she crawled, hands and knees,
along the ground in search of the comb she knew was around

here somewhere. Lord, that rheumatism in her hip joint was acting up!) Then off the fire with the comb, out with the yellowjackets—pop!—and back into a covered iron pan placed in the ashes to crisp. Finally as fine a soup as a body could wish: boil those crispy yellowjackets up in a pot of water with salt and a little bear grease....

All she needed was the yellowjackets. She'd already fetched the water up from the branch in her old iron cook pot, and she'd put up the grease six weeks before from a bear killed by her younger brother Coming Back Tuskateeskee—it'd been browsing among the garbage cans down behind the Pink Motel, and Coming Back, well, his trigger finger itched like an old dog with a lot of fleas. That bear grease was sitting in a crockery jar where the spring shallows up the branch a piece to keep it from going off.

Arminty had just started after a yellowjacket, which, sluggish with spring, was cruising along the forest floor at an altitude of about eight inches, when, pow! Without knowing why or what had happened, the old woman suddenly found herself lying on the forest floor, mostly on her back, but twisted sort of, like a bag of feed fallen off the back of a waggon, and staring up at the big trees that looked down at her the faintly puzzled way big folks do at little ones: "And what do you think you're doing?" There was a smell in her head like a burnt-out blowdryer and sounds too: Zow! Fizz! And it was curiously like that time—and she hadn't remembered this for years—when she'd been a girl tubing down the Oconaluftee with her sister Patrice—this was down around Deep Creek, about five miles up from Cherokee proper—and a storm had blown up all of a sudden—it's like that in these mountains—and lightning struck a field rod grounded in the river. Then Arminty looked over, and what did she see but Patrice seated mid-air, a foot above her innertube, and her braids were standing on end. They looked like the antennae on a bug. And then she had realized that she too was seated mid-air. The two of them got out of that river mighty quick, all right. Only this time Patrice was long dead and Arminty weren't going nowhere, least of all, not quick: she couldn't have moved to save her life.

How long she lay there on the forest floor, she couldn't say. Probably not too long—a moment pinched clean from time, like snuff from a can—but, when the buzzing sounds in her head subsided, and objects swam out of the fog and assumed shapes, and she started noticing what was around her for what it was, the first thing she spotted was the finest patch of slick-go-downs you could ever hope to find, not a foot from where she lay. What luck, thought Arminty groggily. I haven't had no slick-go-downs in a coon's age! Only not for the love of money could she lift her hand to reach the mushrooms. What's wrong with me, anyway? she wondered. True, she had been feeling kind of puny-like this morning, with a beating in her brain, like a second heart pulsing.

That was when her thirteen-year-old granddaughter Nichelle comes crashing through the scrub, as lead-footed as a bear and weighing as much as two. "Granny Quail!" the girl cries out when she sees Arminty, and she plants her hands on her wide hips for emphasis and screws up her eyes until they're no more than slits in her round face. "What are you doing down there on the ground like that!"

Arminty winced. Lord, that child had a loud voice! She could knock a possum out of a tree with that voice—just speaking conversational at it. "I was hunting yellowjackets..." she began.

"And one of 'em stung you? Well, I never! A woman maybe a hundred years old, chasin' yellowjackets!"

"Not one hundred yet, if you don't mind, and in all those years, I ain't never been stung by no yellowjacket yet," Arminty corrected her. "The onliest way I can reckon it is: I must 'a took a fit." She was surprised at how thin and peaked her voice sounded. Keeling over like an overloaded boat. What next? she thought. Then, as Nichelle, with some difficulty and huffing and puffing—for Arminty had some size on her herself; it run in the family—tugged her to her feet, she rallied somewhat and pointed to the mushrooms, "Now, just looky there, Nichelle. Slick-go-downs! You parboil those up, add you a tad of salt, a hunk of grease and a sprinkle of cornmeal...."

"Awh, Granny!" exclaimed Nichelle, making a face.

"What?" Arminty wanted to know.

"Mushrooms!" said the girl with disgust.

"Now, knee deeps. The way you cook them is: you twist off their heads and skin 'em; then you scald 'em. What you have to remember is to hold them under running water all the time you're skinning them or the meat goes real bitter," Arminty told Nichelle.

"I don't like frogs," Nichelle replied. Perched precariously on a three-legged stool, the girl was systematically incorporating into her being a jumbo-sized bag of ketchup-flavoured potato chips. She was a true Tuskateeskee—that was the family into which Arminty too had been born. Her skin was a greenish bronze colour, her hair, chopped short in a modified pixie style, clung to her round head in sooty clumps, and her small, dark eyes were almost oriental in appeerence. She inhabited her 160 pounds with casual awkwardness, as if it were not part of her, but some protective suit of clothing she had donned, like that worn by the goalie on a hockey team. She did not look at Arminty now but sat staring into the fireplace, cold in this season...at the old cast iron cook pot hung from its hook over the ashes of the past winter. Stones being scarce, Arminty's grandfather had woven his bride a fireplace of sticks and clay: grey, tan, yellow, brown, rose, black and red against the grey poplar logs which, hewn on two sides and notched at the ends to fit and hold the corners steady, formed the old cabin's four walls. Above Nichelle's head, hanging from the cabin's darkened beams, dangled bright strings of field corn, popcorn, leather britches and red and yellow pepper, gathered by Arminty and dried before her trouble.

In the month that followed the stroke, Arminty had recovered the use of all her limbs but not her essential strength. Standing for more than a few moments or walking more than the shortest distance was like opening a flood gate—the weakness poured through her limbs like water through sluices. The Big Cove Tuskateeskees conferred on the matter and ended by sending Nichelle to bide with her until she should die. No skin off their noses. With that new youngun of Donella's, there were too many of them over at Big Granny Juanita's place anyhow, and Nichelle, being so altogether large, took up more space than one person had a right to.

Arminty sat on her bed, propped up on feather pillows and covered with a faded quilt, a tall, big-boned woman wearing a green-and-black plaid lumberjacket too short in the arms over a nightgown gone grey and prickly with washing. A bandanna kerchief—blue and white—covered yellowish grey hair, yanked back and twisted into a tight bun at the nape of her neck. She decided to change the subject: "You know my Granny, your great-great-Granny that was called Sally Ann Tuskateeskee, that walked the Trail of Tears when she was just a youngun?" she asked.

"Um." Nichelle, whose mouth was full, was noncommittal.

"Sally Ann was raised up around Sallisaw, Oklahoma, by folks that were not her own," continued Arminty. "Her people died on the trail. A quarter of the nation died on that trail. That's why they called it Nunna-da-ul-tsun-yi, the trail on which they cried. Then, when she was just a couple of years older than you—about fifteen or so—she married Going There Tuskateeskee—he'd gone on the Trail, too, and so folks had taken to calling him that, though it wouldn't have been the first name he'd been called by. Then, just afore the Civil War, he and Sally Ann walked back to North Carolina with about a half-dozen others. A mess of folks did that. Went there and come back. 1200 miles—it's a piece. And that's when my Grandpappy changed his name from Going There to Coming

Back. He said that coming back home was about the most important thing he ever did, and he wanted his name to say that. And his son was called Coming Back after him and his son, your great uncle, and your uncle C.B. too." Arminty fingered the quilt. It was very thin. In some places the light shone through it. "Back then all the designs had names," she said. "Road to Dover, Star of Bethlehem. Broken Star was one of my favourites. This's here's a Drunkard's Path. Granny said the reason she choose it was: Grandpappy didn't draw one sober breath from Fort Gibson to Rattle Snake Springs."

Nichelle shrugged. "It's rotting out in patches," she observed.

Arminty was offended. "It's 130 years old," she said pointedly. "You'd be rotting out in patches too if you were 130 years old."

"Those quilts they have up at the Heritage Outlet?" said Nichelle. "They'll never rot out because they're Of Manmade Materials. When everybody that's in the world is dead and gone, and we're just like the dinosaurs 'cause it's a nuclear wintertime, well, Granny Quail, those Heritage Outlet quilts will still be here. And styrofoam cups and cockroaches too, and they won't have rotted one bit, the quilts, I mean, and I'm talking millions and trillions of years. Because they're synthetic." Nichelle never did say much as a matter of course, but she could talk a blue streak when she was of a mind.

"Thank God I won't be there to see that!" said Arminty and had another stroke.

This time she went away. She couldn't say where exactly, but west, to where the Sun has its tomb, the Darkening Land. It was a long journey there and a longer journey back, and dark, because, the medicine man told her, the Great Frog had jumped up and swallowed the sun and couldn't be persuaded to disgorge it, no, not for anything, and the Great Frog was Our Father in Washington, and his name was Andrew

Jackson, whom the Cherokee call Chicken Snake—it was he who had driven our people from the mountains to a land beyond the Father of Waters.

Stars littered her path—windfall from the meteorite shower that had come five years earlier, an omen to the Cherokee that they had been powerless to interpret at the time. And now all it had presaged had come to pass: removed from the land where the bones of their fathers lay, shorn of all their possessions, they walked this long road in winter. The fallen stars were cold beneath her feet and sharp and hard, like burrs. They tore her tender feet—she had no moccasins, no, nor the wooden shoes her father used to carve his children out of the pine trees that grew up pencil thin and as straight and tall as the sky up around Gregory Bald, because pine is soft, he used to say, like children's feet, but he was dead now. A witch with a beautiful name had taken him: cholera, she was called. That was after smallpox had taken her mother.

And, although Arminty could not see to make out faces, she could see shadows by the firelight and shapes moving through the cloud of her breath. She could reach out her left hand and feel living flesh bump against her fingertips. In the crook of her right arm, pressed against her stomach, she cradled the cast iron pot her mother had given her before she died, saying, "Keep this safe, Sally Ann. You will need it for bean bread."

And the lullabies that put her to sleep were those sung by mothers putting dead children forever to bed in shallow graves chipped from the frozen ground of Tennessee, Illinois, Missouri, Arkansas. She borrowed them, for there was no-one now to sing to Sally Ann.

And she slept fitfully and woke to find that she was no longer Arminty but Sally Ann, and then slept again to wake and find herself Arminty once more, at Yellow Hill, in the bed her grandfather Coming Back had carved out of pine between bouts of drunkeness, under her grandmother Sally Ann's quilt.

"Are you okay?" Nichelle asked uncertainly. She was still perched on the three-legged stool.

Arminty answered, only the words came out mushy. The left side of her face felt frozen, like that time she had gone to the dentist over in Bryson City, and he'd pulled half her teeth out.

"Wharsmapot?" she managed.

"I'll get help," said the girl, jumping to her feet.

"Fetchmemapot!" the old woman called after her, but the girl was out the door and gone.

"Oh, shit!" said Coming Back. He was turning blue, which meant, in Cherokee, that the life was seeping from him in a slow leak, like air from a tire. He had been aware of it for some time. ("Oh, you know! Somebody's probably gone and cast a spell on him," acknowledged Juanita, his mother. "Well, hell. He's kilt enough people.") Now the last thing a man from whom the life was seeping is of a mind to do is to bestir himself on another's account. Still, Arminty was his sister, so he pulled his old toque over his head, saying, "An old man's head is cold even in summer," hauled his miseried bones out of the twig rocker on Juanita's porch and hobbled over to Liza Barkman's ranchstyle home when she and Wally was down in Asheville at a big RV show. Then he broke into their Florida room and stole two of the puppies out of the litter Liza's poodle Bubbles had just dropped. Bubbles bit his hand and his leg. "They may be little, but those poodles got teeth on them like pie-ranas," Coming Back allowed. Then he fetched those puppies over to Yellow Hill.

"You pay attention now, Nichelle, because you may have to do this one day," he told the girl. "First off, you put the puppies in a pot. Give me that pot. Arminty, let loose of that pot."

Arminty had kept a tight grip on the old cast iron cooking-pot since her last fit. Coming Back tugged at it now, and reluctantly Arminty relaxed her grip.

"Ain't you going to kill 'em first?" Nichelle asked, as Coming Back dropped the two whimpering creatures into the pot.

"They'll die soon enough," said Coming Back. "Now, what's important is that their eyes aren't open. If their eyes were open, this here medicine I'm about to make wouldn't work."

He poured a quart of white wine into the pot. The puppies squealed and thrashed and tried to climb out of the pot.

"Get on back down there!" Coming Back ordered them roughly, pushing them back in with the palm of his hand. "Now, you put in...bethany, sage, rosemary, hysops, marjoram, wormwood, camomile and melilot leaves," he said, adding a pinch of each from old Gerber's baby food jars that Arminty collected to fill with the herbs she had gathered in the woods and dried over the ceiling beams. "Now, hog's lard.... It's got to be a hog and make sure that it's white." He ladled some lard on top of the puppies, covered the pot and placed it in the covered pan over the fire. "Now, that'll cook for an hour or so."

"I can't believe that you are stewin' those poor puppies," fretted Nichelle, wringing her plump hands.

"You cain't?" asked Coming Back. Then he settled back in his chair, pulled his toque down over his eyes, and slept for a piece. When he awoke, he took the pot off the fire, poured a good pound of brandy in it, drank the rest of the brandy himself—that was his cut—and strained the mixture in the pot as if he were making jelly, setting the bones and such to one side.

"What do you call that stuff?" Nichelle wanted to know.

"Dog Soup," said Coming Back.

The Dog Soup helped: Arminty got better, though the left side of her face drooped noticeably, and her words remained somewhat slurred. She lingered on without further mishap through that summer and into the fall, and Nichelle continued to care for her up at Yellow Hill in a desultory sort of way. Most of the time the two female creatures ignored one another—this is a highly developed skill among people confined to small spaces. And Nichelle had just come on to her moontime and so, with the loss of eggs and sheddings of blood, had many things to think on and secrets to keep. But sometimes they had conversations:

"I live in the here and now and the future," Nichelle would announce. "So don't you be telling me how to roast no ground hog, Granny Quail, because people don't roast ground hogs nowadays. That's in the past."

"I live in the here and now and the past, and I say my way's better because my past goes back farther than your future goes forward," retorted Arminty. "It goes back to when the earth was soft and wet and very flat, before the Great Buzzard, who was the father of all buzzards after him, flew over this place, and where his wings drooped and struck the mud, there a valley was gouged out, and where his wings flapped up, there a mountain rose. It goes back to when the first Indian woman set her foot down on the Smokey Mountains the Great Buzzard had made with his wings. I can remember back that far. I can. And you know the firstest thing that woman did?"

"What?" asked Nichelle suspiciously.

"She caught her a nice plump groundhog and parboiled it until it was tender. Then she took it out of the pot, sprinkled it with salt and black and red pepper and baked it until it was brown! So there. Now, you remember that, Nichelle, because what's mine to give is yours to take, whether you're of a mind or or not."

"Is that how you see it?" asked Nichelle.

"That's the way it is," Arminty told her.

In the late autumn, Arminty began to slide downhill toward death, impelled by a series of small strokes that picked at her brain like a fastidious vulture. Some parts of her mind it left intact; others it plucked clean out. Bedridden and spun into confusion down the corridors of darkness that led her around and around inside the ravaged landscape of her memory, Arminty rode out a winter that closed in tight as an embrace around the old cabin, a time traveler, straddling centuries. Sometimes an orphaned child, sometimes a young woman, sometimes a crone, but not the same child or the same young woman or the same crone, but always, always carrying the pot. For what mattered was less her identity than the pot itself.

"You don't have to sleep with it," Nichelle would complain. "It's not like anybody's going to steal it, and it's staining the bedclothes all rusty."

"I need it for bean bread," Arminty would mutter. "You can't make bean bread without a proper pot."

Here I am, thought Nichelle glumly: overweight; in Yellow Hill, North Carolina; with a real old crazy woman.

One day in late January, Arminty perked up a tad, and had Nichelle fluff the pillows all up so she could sit and see out the window. It was one of those days when the ground snow is so clean white that the cardinals come out to dance just because they'll look so fine, and there's not one cloud in the blue sky.

Arminty took some Holland gin in a flask, mixed with a little molasses and rainwater. "For my nerves," she explained. "Seeing as how I'm kind of vexious."

"Why are you vexious? Can I have some of that," Nichelle asked, sitting on the edge of the bed.

Arminty passed her the gin. "Well, I reckon I'm going to die soon, and, for the life of me, I can't wrap my mind around it," she said. "In the first place, how'd I come to be old enough to die?"

"Well, you were born about a million years ago," Nichelle pointed out, dragging cautiously on the flask—there was fire within.

"I don't see what that has to do with it," said Arminty. Then suddenly she sagged to one side, then dipped forward and swayed, delineating an almost perfect circle with her torso before snapping upright again. "Oh!" she exclaimed weakly, shutting her eyes tight.

"Lookee here, Granny Quail, if you really are fixing to die, how about you waiting until I can go fetch somebody?" Frightened, Nichelle started to her feet.

"No, no," murmured Arminty, her eyes still closed. She shook her head like she was trying to shake something loose back into place. "I'm all right for now," she breathed. "As for you, you just sit you down and hear me out, 'cause I ain't got all day."

"I don't understand," said Nichelle. "What is it you have to tell me?"

Arminty took a deep breath. "How to make bean bread."

"Oh, Granny Quail!" protested Nichelle. "I don't want to make bean bread."

"That don't matter."

"I don't even like bean bread."

"That don't matter, neither. I ain't saying you're the one I would have chosen, but you're the onliest one here, Nichelle, and I'm going to die afore anyone else comes, so you'll have to do."

So Arminty told Nichelle how to make bean bread. She told her in great detail—how you skin the corn and beat it into meal in the hominy block and work it into a ball and then flatten it and wrap the corn blades around it; how you cook it in hot water in the iron pot. She even made her write the directions down on a piece of paper and fold it up and place it in the battered Bible, at that place in Revelations where it says, "Behold, a door was opened in heaven; and the first voice that I heard was as it were of a trumpet talking with me, which said, Come up hither, and I will shew thee things which must be hereafter."

Then she told Nichelle in a voice thinned to a whisper, "It won't hurt you none to close my eyes, Nichelle. They's a mess of pennies in that blue jar on the shelf." Nichelle was sure glad then that she hadn't spent quite all those pennies, which she had discovered months before, on chips and slushies and jawbreakers, for Arminty died shortly afterwards, and Nichelle used two of them to close her grandmother's eyes.

Arminty Quail had the reputation of being the best Cherokee cook on the Qualla Boundary. She lived to cook the old foods: gritted bread and meat skin soup and lye dumplings and ash cake. Up to the time of her first stroke, she grew all her own vegetables—flour corn for bean bread, leather breeches, cabbage, pumpkin and swamp potatoes. She had her own apple tree and a peach tree too—the peaches were small but sweet as lumps of golden sugar. She harvested the woods around for herbs and mushrooms—di-wa-li oo-ni-ga-di-ge-i, or gingerbread-looking mushrooms, wi si, and deerhorn—and other delicacies, like chestnuts and hickory nuts and possum grapes and ramps, creases and sweet grass, spicewood and sassafras, and cicadas. She baited crayfish with buttermilk in the shallows of the branch, and she began to die hunting yellowjackets for soup.

Nichelle Teesatuskee continued to live in the isolated cabin up at Yellow Hill—there was still no room for her at her great-grandmother's place in Deep Cove, and, besides, she had kind of got used to it up there in the woods. She thought about donating the iron pot to the Cherokee Boys Club when it had that big garage sale in the Spring, but Big Granny Juanita said no. "That pot's been to Oklahoma and back—and it's lasted longer than the ones who took it or the ones that brought it back. Bad luck will come to this family if it goes out of it." So Nichelle hung it back on the hook over the fire where it had hung for 130 years.

All that Spring she dreamed. Dreams of darkness and weeping. Dreams of phantom faces and forms and strange melodies and a bone weariness that she had never in her life experienced. Most of the dreams she forgot, but some she remembered.

One day in July, Nichelle woke suddenly from a dream.

Once again she had been in a dark place with many people weeping. Confused, she rose, and, without thinking, set some beans to boil on the fire. Then she walked out to Arminty's patch on the side of the mountain and picked some flour corn. She shelled it. She went inside the cabin and took the pot off its hook. She carried it outside, poured some water into it, and set it down on the fire she had started in a circle of river rocks. She sifted in some wood ashes and poured in the shelled corn. She sat hunkered down, waiting for it to bubble up. After a while it did. Then she took out a grain and tested it with her fingers to see if the skin was ready to slip. It was. Draining the corn, she washed it in a basket sieve to get rid of the skins. Then she put the corn into Arminty's old hominy block beater and beat it with a heavy piece of wood. When it was fine enough, she poured hot beans into the pan of meal, worked the mixture into a ball, flattened it, wrapped corn blades around the dumplings, folded the ends under and tied them with a strong grass. Then she cooked them in the iron pot out by the branch. She remembered what Arminty had said: not to put salt in them—that makes them crumble. She never had to look at that paper folded up and stuck in Revelations. It was as if Arminty's instructions had been burnt into her brain.

When she squatted down beside the branch and ate the bean bread that she had made, it tasted good. Then, after a piece, she stood and, cradling the cast-iron pot in the crook of her right arm, went inside the cabin, shutting the old wooden door firmly behind her.

Little People Still Live
In the Woods

Mama Jesse Black Crow squatted next to the smoke-darkened hearth, an aged crone with only a scattering of teeth and two knobs for knees under the faded and shapeless calico dress of an indeterminate, earthen colour which she had worn for the last quarter of a century. Bobbing her head like a little towhee bird, she half-sang, half-intoned the ancient formulas connected with birth in a high, shrill whine, breathy with counterfeited urgency: "Hige yu tsa, hige yu tsa, t leki yu, t leki yu...."

"What is she going on about now?" Bethany Whistle

55

hissed into the ear of Ivy Light-Up-The-Sky—Ivy was a midwife, what folks call a Granny-woman. As a consequence, she had had some traffic with Mama Jesse, who was widely thought to be the best Conjure Woman within a hundred miles of the Boundary.

"She's calling the child down," Ivy told the pregnant woman now, settling her back against her pillows and pressing a damp cloth to her feverish forehead. "She's promising him a bow, if he is a boy, and a sifter, if she is a girl. Little boy, hurry, come out! she cries. A bow! Let's see who'll get it! Little girl, hurry, come out. A sifter. Let's see who'll get it!" Ivy smiled. "Works every time." She took Bethany's swollen hand in hers and patted it—Ivy had always been imperious and unrelenting to her own family but was unfailingly kind to strangers. "Now, don't you fret, Bethany Whistle. I know it's been a long time, but there ain't never has been a baby stayed up there forever."

Bethany had been in labour three days, and she was not a young woman. She hadn't got her a man until she was in her mid thirties—too tall and angular, all bones and nose was her problem...and too given to stating her mind. That man was Donnie Spotter, a tight-muscled, weasley kind of small man with an easy humour and an air of detachment that quickly led to him taking off on her. He'd hopped a Greyhound to Cincinnati six months previous , drunk too much Aqua Velva—"As if you could drink too little Aqua Velva!" Nurse Jolly at the infirmary commented upon reading the doctor's letter to Bethany—and now he was about as much company as a telephone pole that drools.

"Brain damage," the Cincinnati doctor's letter had concluded. "Would anybody be coming to fetch him? Otherwise, he'll be locked up in an Ohio state institution, and I can't think of a closer approximation of what shouldn't happen to a dog."

"What shouldn't happen to a dog is a sight too good for Donnie," declared Bethany, who was still spitting mad. "Lock him up and throw away the key. And good riddance to bad rubbish!"

Neverthless, she cried when she reckoned that she was alone and there weren't no-one to hear her. Not much of a man, Donnie Spotter. Still, he had shared her bed and brought warmth to parts of her there was just no pleasing otherwise.

Bethany moaned. Her head fell heavily to one side, her eyelids slid shut over eyes on fire. Nauseated and lightheaded, she could not so much as breathe without pain. The squeeze-squeezing of labour had bruised her ribs; she gasped as they pressed deep into her soft organs. The last two months she'd spent flat on her back in the rickety iron bed, unable to stand without assistance and swelled up like a ka nu nu, like a big bullfrog. Even her ear lobes were distended, and her ankles...her usually bony ankles looked like a fat woman's knees. "Just let it come out," Bethany muttered through clenched teeth. "Dear God. Boy. Girl. Hedgehog. I don't care."

At this, Mama Jesse stopped chanting mid-phrase and slowly turned to look in her direction. Her black eye was cold and opened wide as if to take in the whole of Bethany's swollen enormity. Her evil eye, on the other hand, was shrouded, cloaked, as if the milky cast that hung in it like an exploded star were a smokescreen behind which she plotted. She had fallen on a briar as a girl, a thorn had caught and tore her pupil and in the wake of blindness had come second sight.

Ivy caught Mama Jesse's glance and shuddered. "You mustn't say that, Bethany," she warned the labouring woman. "A witch could be nearby, listening. Then, Lord only knows what might come out of you. I have been a midwife for upwards of ten years now, and, let me tell you, there are things buried in the churchyard up at Yellow Hill that no mother could call a child, and I know 'cause it was me pulled 'em out of folks!"

Turning back to the hearth once more, Mama Jesse inclined forward, and, taking a big iron soup spoon, raked some coals together. She took a pinch of tobacco from a buckskin pouch she wore tied to her belt and dropped it onto the coals. Instantly it flared up. The blue smoke bent to the north, pointing. As Bethany cried out, grasping her shuddering stomach with both hands as if to contain some sudden scuffle within, the conjure woman and the midwife looked up and out the open door beyond the hemlock and the towering cucumber trees toward Thunderstuck Ridge, toward the south. It was summer. A storm hung over the top of Thunderstuck, like black steam off a kettle, like the mountain's black ghost.

"Hit's a witch, all right," Mama Jesse told Ivy evenly— Mama Jesse was not afraid of witches, being one herself, of sorts. "Coming from down yonder off of Old Thunderstuck, from the looks of it." Then, reading Ivy's frightened expression, "No, Ivy. H'aint me." The old woman winked at the midwife...her evil eye. "This here's for hire. You want to dry up a cow? That'll cost you. You want to separate lovers? That'll cost you more. You want somebody to join his ancestors a little in advance of when he might otherwise be disposed to do so? Now, you're talking Big Money," she joked, indicating with a crooked finger the eye with the cast in it. "You know that. Evil Eye tain't never for free."

But Bethany began to grunt like a sow bear—the time had come to push the baby out. Ivy stood quickly and moved to take Mama Jesse's place by the hearth. She reached for her dented copper kettle—a strong tea made with bittersweet and raspberry leaves would soothe the pains of childbirth and milkweed would staunch Bethany's bleeding afterwards— and her big rivercane basket of twice-boiled birthing rags.

As for Mama Jesse, she hobbled peg-legged out of the house and into the clearing. While Bethany pushed and strained, the old woman walked round and round the one-room cabin, smoking a sacred pipe and blowing the smoke in every direction, down every conceivable trail that a witch might use to get to Bethany and the baby in the process of crossing over to their world. "Sge! Uhyu tsa yi galu lti tla tsultahisti," she began in a somewhat conversational tone. She'd tell that witch a thing or two.

"If she don't die, she'll live," was all Mama Jesse would venture regarding the future of Bethany's new baby, Peggie. Peggie didn't look like a hedgehog. For that Ivy was grateful. She did look a whole lot like a big frog, bandy legged and shrunken with an oversized, sad, lolling head. Of course all babies are bandy legged, all have lolling heads, but Peggie's was more bandy legged and her head more sad and lolling than most. Moreover, she was as limp as a mess of cooked noodles and as blue as the moon in a wet winter. Ivy noticed, however, that the child gazed up at her with eyes strangely focused for a newborn as she swabbed her down and swaddled her up, and that they were animated by a fierce, black snap. This made Ivy think that Peggie might live, after all.

The child did live, but she didn't thrive. When she was six months old, Bethany marched her on up to Nurse Jolly at the Cherokee Hospital up near the Mountainside Theatre to have a look-see. The nurse laid her down on a table and moved her legs all around, like she was testing a turkey for doneness by seeing how loose the thigh rode in the hip socket. Then she handed her back to Bethany. "This child has rickets," she told her. "It makes her bones soft. That's why she's all bent out of shape...poor, pitiful creature. That's why she's so splindly small."

"Thank you very much, Nurse Jolly," Bethany said. "But my Peg ain't the least bit pitiful, and she's going to be just fine."

To ensure that, she was very careful to feed the child a strong tea of sage and fern every day for years and years. She even made her sleep on a bed made of the same plants—a sure-fire cure for rickets according to anybody who knew anything— and, to strengthen them, she washed her bowed legs often in saleratus and strong cider.

Four years passed. Peggie's head ran a race with her body and won: her head continued to grow; her body simply stopped. So Bethany took Peggie back up the hill to Nurse Jolly. One look at the stumpy little girl, and Nurse Jolly pursed her thin lips. She didn't care to say, so she called in the white doctor. In her experience he would say just about anything. Sure enough, he took one look at Peggie and said, "What's all this? This child doesn't have rickets. She's a dwarf."

"Well?" asked Bethany.

"Well, what?" asked the doctor.

"Well, what can I give her to treat that?" asked Bethany.

But nobody knew how to cure dwarfism.

Bethany and Peggie lived alone in a little, one-room log cabin in Lost Cove hard by the East Fork of Jenkins Creek north of Highway 19 and Thunderstuck Ridge. Bethany's people had been among those who hid out in the mountains at the time of the Removal. Originally from down around the Spring Place area in North Georgia, they had fled the soldiers of General Winfield Scott who came to round them up and move them out west beyond the Mississippi. They came instead to these mountains where Cherokees have lived since before there were grandmothers to tell of it and threw up this haphazard cabin in some haste before the winter of that sad and dangerous year of 1839 should close in. They were not alone in this. Other, equally haphazard cabins peppered these backwoods, isolated and remote enough to escape the soldiers' notice, but connected one to the other by a network of trails.

So the house had no windows, only a lookout cut next to the fireplace, and its one room was scarce bigger than a goodly corn crib. However, come winter, provided Bethany kept the fire going steady, it was dark and smokey-warm as a bear's cave—it had been well-chinked—and, come high summer, buried in its tangle of blackberry bushes, holly, sassafras, grapevine and sumac, surrounded by its hemlock and its white pine, and with its front and only door propped open to admit a fine view of Thunderstuck Ridge, it was a pretty place to bide. Then Bethany and Peggie would spend their days on the porch and, at night, drag their mattresses out into the dirt dooryard so that they could sleep in the moon's cold wash and count shooting stars as they tumbled to the earth.

Then, one night, when Peggie was about thirteen years old, Bethany told her the story of the Yunwi Tsunsdi and Tsantawu.

"Did you know that there are little people living in hollow trees or rocky cliffs?" she asked.

"No," replied Peggie.

"Oh, yes. They are called the Yunwi Tsunsdi," said Bethany, "and they are no taller than you . They can be kind or not. It depends." She paused. "They are great workers of wonders," she added.

"How do you know this?" Peggie asked.

"My great-great-grandfather was a man named Tsantawu," Bethany told her. "He was not from around here. It was Tsantawu who came here from North Georgia at the time of the Removal, and he brought with him his wife and her mother and his two daughters. He went hunting squirrel one day, but, because he didn't know his way around, he got lost in the mountains on the head of Oconaluftee. It was wintertime and very cold, and everyone thought, 'Well, Tsantawu is surely dead by now.' And his wife mourned, and all the people came to see her. To comfort her."

Bethany rolled onto her back, staring up at the stars. A squinch owl hooted, then dropped from its perch onto some small nocturnal animal like a bomb with claws. The cornlike tassels of the tangled dog hobble lifted in the light breeze, and the moon revved silver like a distant motor. "Sixteen days later," she continued, "up turns Tsantawu! What do you think had happened?"

"I don't know," said Peggie.

"The Little People had found him and taken him to their cave," explained Bethany. "According to him, they treated him well and gave him plenty of everything to eat except...and this is strange...except bread. Oh, they would give him big loaves of bread, but every time he took them in his hand to eat...the loaves shrank. Anyway, after he was okay, they brought him home. As far as Jenkins Creek, that is. When they came to that, they told him,'It is only up to your knees, Tsantawu. You walk across.'"

"But...," Peggie protested, for Jenkins Creek runs swift and deep.

"I know! I know! But that's what they told him," Bethany cut her objection short. "That it was just a shallow creek, and, by that time, he was so used to trusting them that, looking at the creek, he saw it as shallow, even though he knew full well how deep it was. Who knows?" She shrugged. "Perhaps they had cast a spell on him. In any case, Tsantawu crossed the creek, and when he turned to look back, the Little People had gone and the creek had turned back into a deep, swift creek, as it is today, as it has always been. Poor Tsantawu! By the time he reached this house, his legs were frozen to the knees. He lived only a few days."

After some moments thought, Peggie commented, "Tsantawu should have known better. The loaves of bread were a sign—a sign that the Little People would only seem to give him what he needed to live."

"I don't understand," said Bethany, "Why would the Yunwi Tsunsdi trick poor Tsantawu like that? He was only a lone man, a stranger to these woods. He was only hunting food for his family in the winter."

Peggie shrugged. "I think Tsantawu made fun of someone short sometime. Maybe he called someone short a fireplug or a toadstool or 'cocktail sausage' or something like that." (Peggie had been called all of these things.) "Perhaps," she continued, "this was the Little People's way of getting back at old Tsantawu. Remember, a story is not only what you choose to tell, but what you choose not to tell. Tsantawu would not have chosen to tell that part of the story...Perhaps he would not even have thought to tell it. Perhaps he would not have thought it important enough ."

"Possibly," agreed Bethany. " Maybe that was the way it happened."

Peggie Whistle was famous at Cherokee High School because she was the only dwarf most people had ever seen. She became even more famous after she met the starman down beyond Big Witch Gap.

What happened was this: sometimes she went walking in the forest, looking for little people like herself—although she never admitted to that. That was before her dysplasia became so bad she couldn't walk without Canadian crutches. Well, one day she was walking down the trail that dipped through the pine forest from the crest of the ridge toward the bald when she spotted a strange kind of a human-like critter caught halfway up a balsam tree. It was the most peculiar thing she had ever seen. It had a head like a snapping turtle and big blinking, owlish eyes, while its body was akin to a man's, only smaller, and covered with white down that glowed faintly in the gathering dusk."What are you, and what are you doing up that tree?" Peggie wanted to know.

How it talked to her, she never could quite explain. Its voice was curiously bell-like and she heard it, not with her ears, but on the inside of her head.

"I am a starman," it explained to her in this unconventional way. "Drooping low over Heintooga Ridge, I fell and became entangled in the branches of the tree." Something to that effect. "It's not uncommon," it added.

"Maybe you were one of the stars my mother and I watched fall last night," observed Peggie. Then, without further todo, up the balsam tree she shimmied and set about freeing the starman—it was as weak in its limbs and floppy as a baby, which was why its own attempts to free itself had been so futile. Once liberated, it bounced off back into the firmament as if it were sucked there. And that was that.

"No," Peggie told the editor of the Cherokee One Feather who came to interview her about it. "It didn't have no space ship. Not that I could see. Do you want to hear a joke?"

"Sure!" said the editor, who was a game sort.

"Okay," said Peggie. "This is a good one. What did the Indian say when he saw the spaceship land?'"

"I don't know. What did the Indian say when he saw the spaceship land?" asked the editor.

"'Oh, no!'" said Peggie, chuckling, "not again!"

The editor footnoted his piece on Peggie and the starman this way:

"Peggie Whistle is not the first Cherokee to have encountered a starman caught in the trees in some high place. There were several accounts dating from a time before the white man came of hunters discovering creatures answering to Peggie's description of the starman in just such circumstances."

"It seems," he concluded, "that stars have always had difficulty negotiating the zone between heaven and earth."

Bethany died a few years later. A Winnebago pulling out of the Dairy Queen onto 441 backed over her. With the restitution money, Peggie bought an old pickup truck and got herself one of those extensions that make it possible for dwarfs to drive cars—but the pickup never took the place of her mother. Without her, Peggie found herself very lonely in the little cabin up in Lost Cove. She tried becoming a Baptist but reneged moments before her baptism. To tell the truth, ever since her mother had told her the story of Tsantawu, she had entertained fears that water might not be what it seemed, and, besides, everyone knew that waterways were passages to the Lower World.

She took a job down in Chief Saunooke's village on the Oconaluftee making quarters for the tourists who wanted to see Dancing Chicken. Dancing Chicken was a chicken in a cage with an electrified grid for a floor. When a tourist put a quarter in the slot, the grid became active and the chicken first shat from the shock, then capered about like a highland dancer on speed. Peggie liked the job because, when Dancing Chicken died, as it did every week or so, she got to take it home and eat it. Also it gave her a chance to try her jokes out on the general public.

"That'll be twelve quarters," she'd say. "Say, Mister, how would you define a peace treaty?"

"I don't know," the tourist would reply. "How would you define a peace treaty?"

"A peace treaty is when a white man wants a piece of your land!" Peggie would retort. "Hah! Hah!"

Peggie was beginning to get quite a reputation as a joker.

After she had saved up enough money, Peggie drove her truck up to Cinncinnati to pick up her father at the state institution in upstate Ohio where he had lived for the past 25 years. Donnie Spotter turned out to be a shrunken, stooped, shuffling Indian who peed in his pants and took punches at people who weren't there. He also watched nonexistent television, which was okay since the cabin at Lost Cove had no electricity.

The doctor in charge of his ward was incredulous. "Are you sure you want to take him?" he asked the strange looking little Indian woman with the big head and the stumpy body.

"Is the Pope Catholic?" Peggie asked.

"But why?" the doctor pressed. "He's practically a vegetable! He doesn't know you...isn't capable of knowing anything. He's lived here for years. It's going to be quite an upheaval."

"I guess there's just...something about an Aqua Velva man!" declared Peggie. She had been saving that line for years. Sometimes she thought the only reason she had come to fetch Donnie was so that she would have a chance to use it. She felt strangely fulfilled.

Donnie seemed to recognize Lost Cove in a kind of inchoate way. That is, he stared around the clearing, mouth agape, and there was a question...not an answer, but a question in his dull eyes, and a deep V-shaped crease in his forehead just above his nose as if the slow wheels of his mind might be rustily turning over.

"Where...?" he began. He could hardly shift his heavy tongue quickly enough about his slack mouth to speak.

"It's all right," Peggie told him. "I have taken you to my cave here in the woods where you will be safe."

"Who...?"

"I am Yunwi Tsunsdi," said Peggie. "As for you, you are Tsanwatu."

"My name is Donnie."

"No, it's Tsanwatu! And I am Yunwi Tsundi. That means I am a Little Person."

"You are little," Donnie agreed, looking down with her.

"Do you remember Bethany?" Peggie asked.

"Huh?" Donnie stared at her. "Who?"

"Never mind," said Peggie. "I didn't think so. Okay. What about this: I'm going to tell you a joke."

"What?" asked Donnie.

"You ask me, 'Did your ancestors come over on the Mayflower?'"

"Huh?"

"Just ask me."

"What?"

"Okay. Pretend you've asked me. 'Did your ancestors come over on the Mayflower?' And I say, 'No, but they met the boat!' Heh! Heh!"

Donnie didn't get it.

Peggie sighed. "That's okay, Daddy," she said . "You sit up here on the porch and watch some TV."

"What?"

"TV." Peggie steered him onto the porch and sat him down in Bethany's old twig rocker. "TV," she repeated and made as if to turn a knob.

"Oh," said Donnie and settled down to watch the black-berry bush beside the house with an air of contentment.

Peggie watched him. "You don't remember, do you?" she asked him a moment.

"What?" Donnie asked.

"Anything," replied Peggie.

"Huh?"

"All that was important was your own pain."

"Pain?"

"Your pain. Not hers. Not mine."

"I'm trying to watch TV," Donnie pointed out.

Peggie shrugged. "Have it your way," she said. But what she thought was a dark thing.

Although she always appeared cheerful, ready for a joke, Peggie Whistle was an angry woman. She was angry to be an ugly, comical creature, a dwarf, angry too that a Winnebago had backed up over her mother, the one person who had loved her and whom she had loved, angry at the man who had deserted her and her mother and who had not even had the common decency to retain even a measure of sanity, angry that children were afraid of her, that men did not want her, that women laughed at her, and that an accident of birth had doomed her to this solitary life in a place called Lost Cove. There was no-one who would come along and discover her, as she had the bright starman in his tree, no-one to untangle her and set her free so that she could bounce upwards towards happiness. Here and thus must she remain all the days of her life.

Soon she grew tired of Donnie.

Jenkins Creek was running high that year, fed by the snow of the winter before. It took the rope bridge out twice and one of Josiah Etowah's prize milkcows and a baby somebody had birthed but didn't much cotton to.

In late April of that year, it also took the drowned body of Donnie Spotter and rolled it into the rocks down where the creek peters out around Highway 19, like a dog that lays a rat it has caught at his master's feet.

"I don't know. He insisted that he could wade across Jenkins Creek," Peggie told the Cherokee police, Ira Bushytail and Ollie Rattler. "Wasn't that the foolishest thing? It come clean over his head, and he couldn't swim worth shit. Well, everyone knows Daddy was...confused. Sort of like Columbus. You boys know the one about Columbus?"

"No," said Ollie.

"No," said Ira.

They sounded expectant. Everyone knew that the dwarf told good jokes.

Peggie warmed to her audience. "This is a good one," she said. "You ready?"

They nodded.

"Well, you know what they say about Chris Columbus!" Peg began broadly. "He didn't know where he was going, didn't know where he'd been, and did it all on somebody else's money," she said. "Hah! Hah! Hah!" She laughed until the tears ran down her cheeks. Her hip was paining her—a storm was coming on. She could feel it in her soft, twisted bones. "You boys hungry?" she asked. "Like to stay for dinner? Got me a chicken in that pot that done danced his last."

Under Mountain

"Reality is just a construct."

"Who said that?...Answer me!..." Dot Tse struggled to push to one side the weighty darkness blanketing her so that she could sit upright in her narrow bed. Like a child frightened in the night, she drew the sweat-dampened sheets up to the level of her chin and cowered behind the percale shield. "Is...is there anybody here?" she asked in an infinitisimal voice.

No reply.

The shadows loitering in the corners of her bedroom gathered round her, pressing silently in, as the curious will do at the site of an accident.

The same as any other living creature, Winolta Otter had a grandmother, and that grandmother used to tell the young Winolta tales by the woodstove on cold winter nights when the snow that fell cut like glass and the wind yelped and whined outside the cabin up in Paint Town like a pack of wild dogs—if your soul was bare, that lonely, savage sound cut into it like a razor strop—and, though Winolta's grandmother was as fine a Yellow Hill Baptist as you could hope to find, none finer, still these stories that she told Winolta did not mention Heaven or Hell; our Lord Jesus Christ did not figure in them; nor did his Daddy; no, nor his Uncle Devil neither. For these were old stories Winolta's grandmother told her, handed down the generations from Before Times and polished smooth and soft-shiny as river rocks by the thousands of voices that had passed them along. And one of these stories was about Under Mountain.

According to Winolta's grandmother, there is another world, like ours in almost every way. It lies inside the mountains, and for that reason is called Under Mountain. Under Moutain is inhabited by a people much like ourselves, Winolta's grandmother told her. They do not live forever, nor do they always find game when they hunt it, but they live in peace and they need not fear danger. In that they do differ from us. To visit this world is not difficult, but you must fast seven days, and a man must come from there to serve as your guide. There have been those who travel freely between the two worlds, spending time in one, then the other. Eventually, however, a person has got to settle down, and more often than not, he or she prefers to remain Under Mountain, where it is peaceful and safe, and everybody is not as crazy as they are outside.

When Winolta grew to be as old as her grandmother had once been, she fasted. She didn't have much choice. Getting out of bed one day, she had slipped and broken her hip up there in the old Paint Town cabin where she had lived alone since Big Ike

Otter, her husband, had passed over a couple of years before. This was during that bad blizzard we had us a couple of years back, the one that took down the power lines and closed the back roads for going onto a whole week. Well, after Winolta had lain there on the floor beside her bed for seven days, unable to move or, as a consequence, to eat, the big Indian who called himself just Joe but had once been known to her on earth as Joe Light-Up-The-Sky came walking through her door for the first time, picked her up, slung her over his shoulder and took her Under Mountain.

While she was there, an old woman named Maggie gave her a kitten—Maggie's cat had just had a litter, and it is just as hard to dispose of kittens in Under Mountain as it is outside. Wesa was the kitten's name. The white man had introduced the cat to the Cherokee, Maggie explained, and Wesa was the Indians' stab at the English Pussy. "When a cat purrs by the fire, children say it is counting in Cherokee," she told Winolta. "Taladu, nun gi, taladu, nun gi. That means 'sixteen, four, sixteen, four.'" But, of course, Winolta knew this. As for Wesa, he was a scrappy, blue-grey little creature, his ears already ragged from fighting with his brothers and sisters.

At length, once Winolta had returned to her cabin and the floor beside her bed and the roads had been cleared enough so that her grand-daughter Bethany could come visit, her predicament was discovered—not only was Winolta's hip broken, she was also delirious from dehydration and hunger. Bethany admitted Winolta to hospital. Then, as soon as the old woman was discharged from hospital, Bethany admitted her to Laughing Waters Lodge, the Nursing Home on the Oconaluftee on the road to Bryson City. And that was where Winolta had lived for the past two years, with Wesa, the cat that she had brought from Under Mountain.

While Dot Tse, Laughing Waters' resident Reality Therapist, busied herself with a perusal of Winolta's charts, the old woman sat hunched in the chair by the window, balancing a lap desk on her knees. Winolta was a tall, ungainly, comfortable sort of woman in an oversized paisley dress—very useful since gravy stains hardly ever show on paisley, and these days Winolta's hands shook a good deal. With great deliberation, she wrote the following letter in shaky loops on ancient motel stationary:

Dear Mr. Bowdein,
God bless you for the beautiful radio that I won at the Sr. Citizen Luncheon. I am 84 and I live at the rest home. Most of my people are dead except for my grand daughter Bethany who never comes to see me well maybe once a week and its nice to know someone thinks of me. God bless you for your kindness to an old forgotten lady. The woman across the hall is 93 and always had her own radio but would not let me listen to it. The other day her radio fell and broke into a million pieces. It was awful. She asked me if she could listen to mine, and I said Fuck you.
Sincerely,
Winolta Otter
Laughing Waters Lodge, Room 222
Cherokee, N.C.

"Mary Lou! Mary Lou! Please, can I listen to your radio?" the 93-year-old woman across the hall called out in a high-pitched voice as sharp as vinegar.

"For once and for all, my name is not Mary Lou, and no!" Winolta shouted in reply. Then, "Kitty! Kitty!" she called out suddenly, lifting her head and looking sharply in the direction of the bathroom as if she had heard something. "Wesa! Get out of that tub this instant, you bad cat! I swear! We're going to have to get you a litter box, if you keep on messing the tub!"

Dot looked at the bathroom door—she had heard nothing. And there was no tub. Only a shower.

"Winnie, dear," she asked quietly, "who are you talking to?"

Winolta blinked at her, her face blank of expression.

Across the hall, the 93-year-old woman had begun to sing to herself an old Rick Nelson song, "Hello, Mary Lou! Goodbye, heart!"

"Winolta Otter is losing touch with reality," Dot informed David Lowry—the geriatric psychiatrist was a short, spare man of about 40, balding and fussily dapper. They were standing in the foyer of the nursing-home. Dr. Lowry had just arrived from home. He still held his briefcase, bristling with papers. "I suspect she's becoming delusional," Dot clarified.

At Laughing Waters, any change in a resident's behaviour or condition—however inconsequential it might seem—was closely observed and monitored. Dot did not need to be told that, with the Old Ones, little things had a way of becoming big things. An unfortunate accident, for example, might become Incontinence if allowed to continue, or forgetfulness, Dementia. "Laughing Waters Lodge is a progressive facility," as Dr. Lowry had insisted at a recent staff meeting. "Our philosophy is, as much as possible, to nip potential problems in the bud."

"Delusional?" Dr. Lowry repreated. "How do you figure that?" The Inscrutable East, he thought, looking down at Dot. Her flat Oriental face and her thick, child's body.... How could I ever have found her attractive? It was the alcohol, he reasoned. On all three occasions.

"She thinks that blue plush cat of hers is real," Dot explained. "She talks to it. Says things like, 'Here, kitty, kitty!' and 'Stop that, bad cat!'"

"Hmmm!" murmured Dr. Lowry.

"David?"

"Yes?"

Dot lowered her voice. "Have you spoken to your wife yet? I need to know."

An expression of pain flickered across Dr. Lowry's face: the shadow of a bat's wing laid across a moonlit sweep of ground.

"Now is not the time or place, Dot," he advised her solemnly, in a tone that informed her of his grave displeasure. Turning smartly on his heel, he strode down the hall toward the east wing.

Stricken, Dot waited. Then she also headed down the hall, stopping at the locked washroom marked Staff to throw up the dry toast she had eaten for breakfast. She was two months pregnant with Dr. Lowry's baby. When she had told him about it three weeks before, he had promised to get a divorce and marry her. So far...or so Dot gathered...he hadn't broken the news to his wife.

"I'm so lonesome without my radio I could die!" crooned the 93-year-old woman across the hall . "Oh, please, please! Can't I borrow your radio just this once? Mary Lou?"

"I'm not Mary Lou, and you could die any minute, with or without that radio. You're 93 years old, Joella Red Deer!" Winolta reminded her. "That woman!" she exclaimed to Dr. Lowry. "I'll have you know I won that radio fair and square at the Sr. Citizens' Luncheon, Dr. Lowry. I drew the lucky ticket."

"You couldn't share?" Dr. Lowry asked.

"Sharing's for three-year-olds," Winolta informed him. "What's mine is mine."

The geriatric psychiatrist sat in the chair by the window. Winolta sat opposite him. In her lap she held a blue plush cat that was missing one black button eye. She stroked the stuffed toy absently.

"I'd like to talk to you about your cat, Mrs. Otter," Dr. Lowry began.

"I'm not getting rid of it, if that's what you're on to," Winolta informed him.

"No, no. Not at all," Dr. Lowry assured her. "What I'd like to know is...would you say, Mrs. Otter, that your cat is.... Ahhh! Real?"

"Real?" Winolta echoed faintly. She was peering out the window at a young man shoving a lawn mower up and down the stretch of river bank. "Real?" Now, there was a slice of sweet tater pie, if ever I saw one, she thought. Big, good-looking boy. Isn't he one of those Rollover kids of Lucille's? "What do you mean by real?" she asked Dr. Lowry.

"Alive," Dr. Lowry clarified.

"Ah! Alive!" echoed Winolta. She leaned forward in her chair, nearer the window to get a better look. The sight of a man's strong, bare back...the knitting of the muscles there...never failed to send an ache shimmering through her groin. Oh, you never do lose the taste for it, she thought. No. Not ever. I'll be on my dying bed, and the way a man's parts fit together'll be the last thing I think of. So help me, God, but you made a thing of beauty when you made a beautiful man. Now, a homely man.... She looked at Dr. Lowry with contempt. Such a fussbudget, she thought! She bet his penis was this big.

"Yes," he encouraged her. "Alive!"

Winolta laughed—it sounded like a bark. She felt so dreamy all of a sudden. She wished Doctor Lowry would go away so that she could crawl into bed and fantasize about the boy outside. She drop-kicked the stuffed toy cat in its plush stomach. It flew a few feet in the air, landing softly before the door to the hall.

This woman is about as delusional as I am, concluded Dr. Lowry. He stood. Dot is losing it, he thought. It's the stress. She's reading psychosis into the most inconsequential things. He walked toward the door. What a fool he had been to get involved with her. Anyone could see how desperate she was, how close to the edge. And what had happened to the sixties, anyway? Didn't women use birth control any more? Of course, he reckoned, it could be an hysterical pregnancy. Dot was just the sort to have an hysterical pregnancy—a not very pretty woman in her mid thirties...you could hear her biological clock ticking in Swain County, and there was this look in her eyes.... She was famished for love. If I do nothing, he told himself, take no action whatsoever, it may just blow over.

As his hand closed around the doorknob, Winolta emerged from her reverie in time to say, "Oh, Doc!"

"Yes?" Dr. Lowry turned around.

"Let the cat out on your way, would you?" Winolta asked.

Dr. Lowry, Dot Tse and Winolta Otter sat in Winolta's room. The way the psychiatrist and the reality therapist had placed themselves made Winolta feel as if they were the Indians and she the fire. You have it wrong, she thought. I am the Indian here. She didn't like the way they were looking at her: intently, as people do when they gaze into flames—either because they are fascinated by the fire, or because they believe they will see something there. She clutched her blue plush cat tightly to her breast.

"That's a pretty pussy you have there," Dot commented.

"You think so?" Winolta asked. Holding the toy at arm's length, she surveyed it critically. "He's lost an eye," she observed. "I 'pect in a fight. Tomcat, you know. He's always been a scrapper."

"I'm just curious, Mrs. Otter," Dr. Lowry said. "Just how is it that you've managed to feed your kitty all this time. I mean...cats aren't generally allowed at Laughing Waters Lodge. Do they sell cat food in the Little Store?" The Little Store was just off the Common Room.

Winolta paused. She had to admit that he had her there. She tried to remember back to the last time she had actually opened a tin of Nine Lives, scooped its rank-smelling contents into a dish, or, indeed, if she ever had. "Well, to tell you the God's truth, Dr. Lowry, I don't know what he lives on," she confessed. But it is summer, she reminded herself. The cat was out of doors a good deal. Probably he caught mice. Or bats. Cats were good at fending for themselves.

"Does he breathe?" Dr. Lowry asked a second question.

Winolta lifted the cat gently so as not to wake it. She held its chest to her ear and listened to his contented burr of breath for a moment. Then she smiled gently and nodded. "Yes," she said softly. "Yes, he does."

Dot Tse taped a piece of paper to Winolta Otter's door. In the handwriting of a very precise child it read:

Mrs. Otter is in Reality Therapy. Please ask her:
The day of the week
What year it is
Who you are
Who the current president of the United States is

"I don't understand," Winolta's granddaughter Bethany said. It was Thursday, her day to visit.

"It's just that your grandmother's short-term memory has begun to deteriorate," Dot explained. "Probably she's suffered a series of minute strokes. As her long-term memory remains intact, she will tend to live more and more in the past. Because it's more comfortable for her. More predictable. It's like having a lazy eye. You know. You tend to favour it to the other's detriment. Well, in your grandmother's case, she has a lazy short-term memory." She smiled blandly. She was on her fifth librium of the day. It was 11.30 in the morning. The air around her felt as thick and absorbent as cotton batting. The floor absorbed her footfalls like a giant sponge. I'm all right, she thought, marvelling.

"Let's get this straight," demanded Bethany. "You're saying that, even as we speak, lights are going out all over my grandmother's head?"

"That's right," said Dot, nodding.

"If that's the case," argued Bethany, who had a combative nature, "what the geezley good is it going to do her to know that Ronald Reagan is the President of the United States?"

"It's George Bush, Mrs. Whistle, and the goal of Reality

Therapy is to orient a person to time, place and person." It was a litany, and Dot intoned it as such.

"That don't answer my question," persisted Bethany. "What good does it do her?"

"As health professionals, our job is to keep our patients functioning at their best level physically and mentally," Dot recited.

"Humphf!" Bethany contended. She turned away from Dot and knocked once on the closed door. At Winolta's "Come in!" she entered. Dot attempted to follow her. "I'd rather speak to my grandmother alone, if you don't mind," she told Dot.

"Well.... okay!" conceded Dot. "But, remember! Ask the questions!"

Bethany shut the door in her face. "Hello, Grandmother," she greeted Winolta.

"Hello, Bethany," Winolta greeted her in return.

"You recognize me?"

"I'm not blind yet," Winolta pointed out.

"Grandmother?"

"Yes?"

"What day of the week is it?"

"Thursday. It's Thursday because that's when you come visit me, isn't it?"

"Yes," said Bethany. "Grandmother?"

"What, Bethany?"

"Just who is the President of the United States these days?"

Winolta shook her head. "You know, a couple of people have asked me that just today. You should know these things, Bethany. It's your responsibility as a citizen. Do you know how hard it was for Indians to become citizens?"

"There's nothing wrong with my grandmother," Bethany told Dot upon leaving. Just then Winolta called out, "Truman! Harry S. Truman. Would you believe that it slipped my mind there for a moment? And, Bethany?"

"What, Grandmother?"

"Let out the cat, why don't you?"

On her day off, Dot Tse, who was on her way to Knoxville to buy baby things, found herself stuck in a bear jam on Highway 441—a bear jam occurs when a bear wanders out onto a shoulder of the road and a tourist stops his car to take a photo, backing up traffic behind him sometimes for miles. That is, thought Dot, parked uneasily behind the steering-wheel of her Ford Escort, it could be a bear jam, or it could be an accident, one of those Winnebagos that periodically and spontaneously combust on the twisty, steep road through the National Park. She felt the panic rising and immediately began to breathe as her own therapist had suggested she ought in situations like this—deeply, rhythmically—all the while praying that she might make it through this traffic tieup without having a panic attack: Dear God! Over the past couple of months being stuck in traffic had triggered at least a half-dozen such attacks, some quite severe. She glanced at her rearview mirror. Stuck to it with scotch tape was one of the cards that had come with the relaxation tapes her therapist had ordered from California. The instructions explained that the cards were aides memoires: they reminded you of what a calm, confident person you in fact were, despite the reality that you might at any moment succumb to a totally inexplicable panic attack. Reality is relative, Dot reminded herself. The particular card stuck to her rearview mirror read, "A calm centre."

Reaching into her purse, she pulled out her bottle of librium and swallowed two. Then she pulled over to a scenic lookout and lay down on top of a picnic table there, flat on her back to do the special kind of deep breathing. A quarter of an hour later, a tourist from Brampton, Ontario spotted her lying there, pulled off the highway and came to her assistance. He thought she was in labour.

While in Knoxville, Dot purchased a crib and a car seat at Toys 'R Us. She had consulted Consumers' Guide beforehand to determine which features to look for and what makes were the very best. Both items were expensive, so she put them on her credit card, bringing herself to within a few dollars of her limit. That was okay, she told herself. Doctors made wonderful salaries. The crib came unassembled, which was just as well because that way she could slide it under her bed. The car seat she put in her hall closet. It was seven months until the baby would be born, after all, and she only had the one-bedroom apartment. Later she and Dr. Lowry would be together. They would have a big ranch-style house with a nursery and possibly a live-in nanny from the Philippines. Dot didn't trust the Indian girls. What she needed was a nice Philippino.

"When Dr. Lowry marries me, things will be all right," Dot assured herself, between deep rhythmic breaths.

"When Dot has the abortion, it will be like it was before," said Dr. Lowry.

"When I achieve life balance, I will be an integrated person," added Dot.

"That is," Dr. Lowry reflected, "if she is really pregnant at all, which I doubt."

Several weeks later, Winolta began to positively pick at her food. Later, she stopped eating altogether. "It bores me is all," she told the nurse. Dr. Lowry ordered her put on an intravenous drip. Then, shortly afterwards, on a Thursday afternoon at three o'clock, Winolta had a visitor.

"Congestive heart failure," was how Dr. Lowry named the visitor.

"The goddamned Angel of Death," was the way Bethany described him. She had been sitting by the bed when it happened."I felt his wings graze my scalp." And, sure enough, the hair fell out where his wings had brushed her, and it never did grow back. For the rest of her life, Bethany had a bald spot in the shape of a crescent on the top of her head.

Winolta, however, saw her visitor as a man who was by this time quite familiar to her, a middle-aged Cherokee, handsome, tall, shambling and shuffling, with a fire-spot in one eye and a bit of a belly on him. Joe was his name. "I thought you'd might want to visit Under Mountain," he told her. He was not at all adverse to carrying Wesa in his arms, but they had something of a discussion about whether to take the radio she had won at the Senior Citizen's Luncheon. "Reception is not so hot in Under Mountain," Joe reminded her, and finally she agreed to leave it.

Joe took the old woman from Laughing Waters Lodge to the side of Mt. Noble, where there is a cave. To those who have not fasted, who have no guide, the cave was just that: a cave, but to Winolta and Joe, it opened out like a great door in the side of the rock. Beyond the great door rolled an open country and a town, with houses ranged in two long rows from east to west. The houses were a little old fashioned. Cabins, really, like those up around Yellow Hill. Of course Winolta knew what to expect, because she had been Under Moutain before. Temporarily at least she would stay with Maggie, the woman who had given her Wesa in the first place. Her cat had had another litter. The place was crawling with kittens.

Surveying the prospect, Winolta, though weary from the journey, sighed with relief. "You know, I think I'll stay this time," she told Joe, taking the cat from him. "Out there, everybody is crazy."

Bethany didn't want Winolta's radio. She did not cotton to popular culture. She did want the cat. "Where is it?" she asked.

Wesa was nowhere to be found.

In the end, it was the 93-year-old woman across the hall who got Winolta's radio. She thought it was her old radio, the one which had fallen and smashed into a million pieces. "Fixed!" she exclaimed to the nurse. "About time." Turning it on, she adjusted the dials to pick up WKTC, the country station out of Waynesville.

Star Feathers

We are memory, rough-edged with a pain that time will smooth to something sweeter....

That's what he had written on the flyleaf of the book he had given her—Nick Coughtry, the white man/poet for whom she had left her white man/Marine husband. June Lily laid the inscription before her grandmother with the same proud earnestness as a dog presents its master with a murdered rat: here! Look what I have caught! See what I am capable of!

Reading the pretty words, old Ivy Light-Up-The-Sky

snorted like a horse, hacked like a dog. "Star feathers," was all she said.

June Lily heard the news two days after Dennis left for Camp Lejeune with the kids. Her friend Angela, also a schoolteacher, called her on the phone and said, "Are you sitting down?"

"I'm crouching," replied June Lily. She had already moved the furniture to the new apartment. The house where she and Dennis and the children had lived for the past three years was empty, her old life dismantled and in boxes.

"You aren't going to like this," Angela warned her. She hesitated, then, "Nick has left his wife and gone off with another woman. Some kind of journalist. He's gone to Orlando, June Lily."

"Nick?" June Lily whispered her lover's name, incredulous. "Orlando? To Disneyworld?"

"No, June Lily. To live." Angela was triumphant. She hated Nick. She hated the fact that June Lily had broken up her family, left her children for him. This was something Angela would never have done.

"Oh, God," murmured June Lily.

"Are you all right?" Angela asked.

"I knew he would leave his wife," said June Lily. "Just...not so soon. Not before I was ready."

"Well, it's typical, isn't it?" Angela said, then, after a moment's pause, "Are you all right?"

"Yes," said June Lily. This time the voice she spoke with was not her own. It must have been her mother's or her grandmother's. June Lily knew that because she spoke with an Indian voice, and, over the years since she had flown the Boundary on the wings of higher education and consolidated her exile by marrying Dennis, she had made herself by slow degrees a white woman. "Goodbye," she continued in this Indian voice. Carefully she replaced the receiver in its cradle, continuing to kneel. She remained in that position for a moment. My God! she thought. And I let Dennis take the children! Then she pitched forward onto her hands and began to scream.

Three minutes later Angela called back. "I knew you weren't all right," she informed her.

The following day June Lily, Angela and another teacher from their school went for a walk in the forest. June Lily remembers how it was: cold and clear. There had been an ice storm the night before. As June had knelt screaming, as her children had lain weeping in unfamiliar beds, reaching out their small arms to their father and saying, "Daddy, I forget what Mommy looks like!" and Dennis saying, "She looks like Tiger Lily in Peter Pan. She looks like Pocahontas in your schoolbook," the rain had fallen, then frozen, and the branches of these Northern trees sparkled in the sun like something cheap and beautiful. When the wind ran its hard fingers through them, they made a rattling sound, hollow, like the dried bones of birds.

Nick had not liked children. He wouldn't have taken her with children, and she had loved him so much.... She had bought her freedom from Dennis with her children, traded them for the possibility of Nick and now.... No children. No Nick. If I think about this, I will die, June Lily told herself.

In the wash of raw light her friends looked older than June Lily thought of them as being. Were those lines around Angela's eyes? Was Nadine going grey? Each one's life was in some measure a burden she bore, but still she shouldered it, ploughed on. Knew what direction she was going in even. Not June Lily. Not now. Last year, even six months ago she had been all right, but events had brought her to her knees. Well, who knows? Angela and Nadine thought. Perhaps it will be my turn next. The death of a parent. A child's fatal illness. Poor June Lily. Such a stupid accident, really, breaking her heart when she needn't have bothered. Secretly they formulated a cultural explanation. June Lily, exotic, naïve, too trusting. For all her education, an Indian girl just off the reservation. Everybody but her had seen what kind of man Nick Coughtrey was. Not in a million years would he have gone with her. Yet she had sacrificed her children for him! It was pathetic beyond words.

"I never did see what you saw in him," Nadine said now. "Short, with piggy little eyes."

"I've always said he was a shit," agreed Angela. "Never once have I said that he was anything other than a complete shit and an utter bastard. One! Two! Three!" she prompted Nadine.

"Nick Coughtrey is a shit!" they cried in unison.

They were so loud that tobogganers on the nearby hills stopped to stare at them.

"Do you feel better now?" Angela put her arm around June Lily and gave her a squeeze. "You know you're better off without him."

"I know" said June Lily truthfully. "And I feel better."

And June Lily did feel better...for the moment. Later, however, she went home to the empty house—all that space which had once been filled up with her life, with her children's lives, that she had emptied so that there would be room in it for Nick. She felt vulnerable in such a void, exposed to elements—not wind, not rain, but fear, regret. I cannot think about the children! she thought. I will go mad if I think about the children! Going into the bathroom, she squeezed herself into that narrow space between toilet and wall and there waited out the night that was all around her and dark, like a high and unprotected place.

"Whatever you do, don't leave," she had said to him, reaching out to grasp his elbow as he rose from the bed. To detain him. Not just that once, but on principle. He hadn't answered then. He had made no promises. Now he was gone.

"You'll come with us. You're our Mommy, and you won't leave us," Matthew had told her as she put him to bed on that last night. Polly, older, lay weeping in the next bed. "You'll stay and be our Mommy forever." She hadn't answered then. She made no promises, just disengaged her fingers from his grasp. What she was doing was incomprehensible to him. He couldn't take it in. How she could pack their clothes, send toys ahead. The singlemindedness of her sacrifice. I love him, don't you see? They didn't see.

Now June Lily's many white friends worry about her. What seemed simple now appears complex. The pain hasn't passed with time, as they expected it would. As it ought. There is a feeling in her chest. She compares it to broken glass.

"It's been months!" they say to one another. "Surely it's the children she mourns." They hate to believe otherwise—that June Lily is so unfeeling as not to miss her children. Why, in her place.... "Think what she has given up! This fuss over Nick Coughtrey.... It's just displacement."

In the meantime June Lily studies old newspaper clippings about the poet and his work, contemplates violence. She takes out the few photographs she has of him and stares hard at them, trying to reconstruct from bare likeness the living face. "He looks like Peter O'Toole on a bad day," she finally decides. "How can I love this man? Nevertheless...."

Sheathing the photos in polyurethane, she puts them carefully to bed in the scented darkness of her lingerie drawer. The books he has written are there too. Photos and books, cave creatures dreaming black and white dreams, caught in a charmed sleep among the sachets and the lace—that is how white she has become behind her brown skin: she fills her drawers with sachets and lace and relics of old lovers. Nick's haggard face uncovered momentarily as she lifts the slip from the drawer; the catch of his hooded eye as she reaches for her panties.

Whenever June Lily gets into a car, she cries. Every single time. It's becoming annoying. What is it about cars?

Nadine teaches geology. She put it this way: "June Lily's surfaces are soft, but not as porous as we may have thought. Pain cuts a deep channel through her."

But Angela says, "See here, June Lily, I'm sick of this nonsense over that good-for-nothing man. It's time you saw a therapist."

June went for crisis counselling with Bella Bonner. Bella was a large-bosomed woman in a dress patterned with hibiscus— she specialized in Grief. "I was a Methodist minister," Bella told June Lily. "Then a drunken driver totalled my car. Of the five people involved, I was the sole survivor. I realized then that life is a miracle, that I had been spared for some purpose." This is where June Lily fitted in.

"What we are dealing with is after image," Bella explained. "This man actually was in your life for only a very short time and he passed entirely out of your life months ago. He has no reality for you, yet he haunts you. He is like a ghost caught in the mirror, a shadow on your heart. He requires exorcism if you are to be free to worry about what is real—your extraordinary sacrifice of your children."

"I thought you were a Methodist," said June Lily.

"Symbolic action," Bella ignored her. "How about this? You take Nick's first chapbook, that one written fifteen years ago. It has that poem on that waterfall in it...you know the one I mean. You go to that waterfall. You take the book with you. You stand on the cliff overlooking the waterfall, close your eyes, and you invest, I mean, really invest that book with Nick. Then you open your eyes and look at the book, and you cry, 'Goodbye and good riddance to you, sea cucumber of a man!' and straightaway you fling it into the falls. She looked expectantly at June Lily. "Well?" she asked. "It's your chance to express yourself."

"I don't know that I want to express myself exactly," explained June Lily. "I just want to stop crying in cars."

"Life is a dance, replete with gesture!" declared Bella.

87

"That waterfall's all the way over in Pelham Country," June Lily pointed out. "That's a ways from here."

"What you need is an outward manifestation of an inner movement," Bella advised. "I'm talking about rejection enacted. You've got to wash that man right out of your hair."

"He inscribed it for me," June Lily said.

"Your hair?" asked Bella.

"No," said June Lily, a bit annoyed. This was costing her money. A lot of money. "The chapbook."

"Well? So much the better. You're letting go of something of value to you, after all. It's not supposed to be easy, June Lily. Dealing with inner conflicts never is."

"It won't work," said June Lily.

"If you don't think so...," Bella sounded huffy. "You don't have to do it. It was only a suggestion."

June Lily knew then that she had hurt the big woman's feelings.

The new apartment was on the sixteenth floor and looked south over the city. Below June Lily were the railroad tracks. She liked to stand on her balcony and watch the trains pass far below. Orlando, Florida was somewhere down that track.

I am point A, and he is point B. The railroad track is the line between point A and point B. It connects us.

June Lily taught Math.   Sometimes in the early hours of the morning she would wake to the sound of a train passing. She would startle from her sleep and whisper, Nick! The line curved like a bow, the two points meeting....

It was hot July and still.

Aureoled in spray, glum, June Lily stood on the rocky point overlooking the falls in Pelham County. Streams of water glinted like the teeth of a silver comb over the jagged spur of escarpment. Below her, far below, sunlight reflected off the water, played on the weather-stained surface of the opposite cliffside like fire on the arc of a night's cave, and the hot river glided green and snake-like, a slow insinuation down into the earth.

I am here, she thought, feeling sweaty and put upon. It had taken her an hour to get to this place by uncertain roads, and now there was a Mennonite couple lying together in a grassy knoll not ten feet away. They were lying on their backs with about a foot between them. The boy had placed his black hat on his stomach and was chewing a hayseed. The girl lay rigid on her back, at attention with her arms held tightly to her sides, her toes in their high-topped black boots pointing towards the sky. They were looking at June Lily. She knew it. She could feel the auger of their gaze bore into her back. It was as tangible as the faint breeze that blew up from the forest of dried cedar. They wanted her gone. They wished her away. They had plans, and the Indian woman standing on the cliff was not part of those plans. Could she wait them out? Chances were their need was more pressing that hers. She had come to please Bella, they to please themselves.

Best make it quick, she thought. She pulled the chapbook out of the satchel. What will they think if I abruptly fling a book into the falls and stalk off? she wondered. One thing for certain. She couldn't say, "Goodbye and good riddance, sea cucumber of a man!" Not with Mennonites in heat watching. Just as well. Where had Bella come up with the sea cucumber comparison? she wondered. Oh, yes. June Lily had once compared him to that species of holothurian—tough, slippery, insensate.

She glanced at the tattered cover of the chapbook. Once, at the beginning, she had read his poetry until her mind bled his images. She had hoped he would write about her as he had his wife, that love would move him to this. When she lost faith in that happening, she became unable to read his work. The poems taunted her. They bit into her heart with the twin teeth of a snake. And now....

She opened the book to the flyleaf. For June Lily. A knife slipped between the bones.

How can I kill with mere intention something with so developed a root system as my love for him? she thought. It grows up through me. It binds the bits of me together. She closed the book. In an agony of leaden dullness, she squeezed it to her breast and closed her eyes against the sight of all that water falling, falling. Nick, suspended in a solution of print, in a poem written long ago when he was young and upcoming and new.... The only piece of him that I can hold.... I can't put it from me, she thought.

She turned to walk away. She felt the Mennonite couple shift as she did. The boy rose to one elbow.

For June Lily, she thought. Time will smooth to something sweeter.... Not much of an inscription.

As she picked her way along the dry dust path, the cedar in the breeze made a sound like the whispered conversation of taffeta skirts with hardwood floors.

It was fall now. A lingering death. From the balcony of June Lily's apartment, she could see trees on the distant hills robed in brilliance.

The shirt of fire Medea had given to the Corinthian bride of Jason, she remembers. Children sacrificed there too. No revenge for June Lily though. Just blood on her hands and life going on in its crippled way. Tap-tap-tap, the cane against the pavement. June Lily sighed. Her love for Nick had grown so threadbare now.... Like a piece of cotton washed over and over again. Wrapped around her shoulders, it no longer kept her warm. Taken into her hands, it hung in shreds. The beds where love is made are like deserts of shifting sand, she thought. They throw up mirages. Once she had taken Nick into her body, he had seemed transformed to her. He had seemed opportunity, a way out of the labyrinth, when, in fact, he was nothing but himself. And what was that? June Lily shrugged. She would never know now. All this for nothing.

A train pulled into the station. Royal Blue and canary. A passenger train.

I could throw the chapbook over the railing, thought June Lily. I can do it now. What difference does it make, his 'For June Lily' A face I can't reconstruct from photos, memories that are like dreams. Our substance, his and mine together, is something light shines through; it is shadow. He is with another woman now; there is no more us.

June Lily, standing on tiptoe, peered over the edge to the point sixteen floors below where the chapbook would land. It was a slim volume of non-verse. It must weigh only a few ounces at most. What would be its impact on landing? There was a clause in her lease which stipulated that no tenant hurl objects from the balcony because of the danger to pedestrians. June Lily sighed and straightened up. No, she decided. Whatever happened or failed to happen between Nick Coughtrey and me is not a good enough reason to murder some unsuspecting passerby with a plummeting chapbook.

Later Bella would say that this incident showed that she was coming out of it: "Concern for the Unknown Other...."

June Lily wrote Dennis, asking if she might visit the children.

Dennis wrote back, refusing. "At first they cried every night, wanting you. Now, they don't so much. It drove me crazy for a while. I don't want them starting up again, June Lily. Best for all concerned that they forget you."

When school was out for the summer, June Lily handed in her resignation to her principal, loaded her belongings into a U-Haul trailer and drove home to Cherokee, North Carolina and the Qualla Boundary.

A few days after she arrived, Ivy Light-Up-the-Sky, her grandmother, told her this story there on the porch up at Deep Cove. She told it with a purpose. "Many years ago," the old woman began , "a warrior with a penchant for wandering went down into the white settlements toward the east. There he saw a peacock for the first time. His wonder at this bird was so great, that before he returned to his mountain home, he traded something of great value for a few of its beautiful feathers. These he made into a headdress.

"At the next dance held by his village," she continued, "he wore the new headdress and told all who would listen that he had been up to the sky and that these were star feathers. Everyone believed him at first." She shrugged. "Eventually, he was found out."

"Is that the end of the story?" asked June Lily after a moment. She had grown used to white man stories during her sojourn in their eastern settlements—these end with great and clear finality, while Indian stories merely break up like fights or modulate like music into a different key or drift away like smoke.

"Yes," said Ivy, looking offended. She was known as a good story teller, someone who could drive a tale straight and true—like a nail into the heart of soft wood.

The next day, June Lily drove the two hours into Knoxville where there is a Rare Books Store. "How much is this worth?" she asked the store's owner. She showed him Nick's chapbook.

He took it from her, opened it, studied the flyleaf. He knew Nick's name. The world of successful poets is a small one. "$400," he said. "It's not in bad shape. There was a run of a hundred...."

"And the mice ate a box of 25," finished June Lily. She knew the story.

"Are you sure you want to part with this?" the bookstore owner asked. "If you hang onto it for a couple of years...."

"I've finished it," said June Lily.

"Poetry you can read over and over again," the bookseller pointed out.

"Only if it makes any sense," replied June Lily.

"Well, okay," the bookseller acquiesced, and he took out his chequebook. "Can't say I'm sorry to take it off your hands. Be sure to have a buyer."

June Lily never did go back to the white settlements. Instead she took a job as a Math teacher at the Cherokee High School—they had never had such a fine Math teacher before. During the evenings of that first year back she learned how to double weave baskets in the lightning pattern from Talahina Bluebird, a friend who had once been wild but had become with the passage of time and the acquisition of many pounds, a solemn Keeper of Traditions. The art of basketry soothed June Lily as it has soothed lunatics for centuries. She told Talahina, "I feel that, with my fingers, I am weaving the fibers of my torn heart together...to make a tighter seal." Talahina understood such things all too well. "That is why we women have always worked with our hands," she told June Lily. "Things are forever unravelling and it is up to us to tie up the loose ends."

June Lily began to grow her black hair long and wear it in braids.

Two Christmases after she left him, Dennis sent her the children. He sent them to her for good. He had found a new woman, and she was not interested in raising his two half-breed children.

The story of June Lily's terrible grief ended the way an Indian story often does. Over time, it simply dispersed, like a crowd which, once the worst is over and there is no more to be seen, drifts away.

Rabbit's Foot

Crunch. Snap. Drag. Reuban Rollover was not one of those
Indians who never makes a sound when he walks in the woods.
The forest sagged and squeaked under his heavy tread like a
whorehouse mattress during peak hours on a Saturday night.
Naturally the rabbits could hear him, even though their council house lay at a distance of over five miles—all the way round
the north side of Cades Cove in the place called Tsisduyi,
Rabbit Place. The heavy footfall. The drag of the bag. Because
the earth's crust is like its skin. What's inside knows what's

outside. It can feel it. And rabbits, even those who have passed beyond to Usunhiyi, the Darkening Land, have big ears.

"Shit," snapped one of them now, glancing sharply upwards.

"That man Rollover is at it again," noted another with exasperation.

These rabbits are spirits, nunnehi, long dead, but, like all men and animals, dead and alive, they have their council houses, their tribes and their ball games. They live here, under the hard pate of Gregory Bald to the west of the Boundary; their spirit bodies flash, like sheets of heat lightning, through the dark tangle of roots and worms that is the mountain inside. And like all spirits, they have a tendency to brood; to nurse grievances as if they were litters of young. That's because it's a dark thing, passing over. Being at last a dead and not a living thing. It makes everyone to whom it happens nervous.

"What's to be done?" they all asked now, turning to the Great One, who resembles them but is an altogether bigger creature. It is said that he comes from out West and was actually a jackrabbit when he was alive. "That Reuban Rollover never begs our pardon," the rabbits pointed out. "Not once. He doesn't cover the bones of our dead with presents as by rights he ought. It is the ancient law." They are such sticklers for protocol. "There's no atonement," they complain. "We insist that the rules be enforced."

The Great One surveyed his tribe. They are like shadows, half glimpsed; like candles guttering. Their voices hang on the air like blown pollen. "If you insist, what am I to do?" he acquiesced, shrugging.

That same year, Reuban's daughter Molly was born sooner and smaller than she should have been; she never thrived. But the winter she was three, she took a decided turn for the worse: she sickened and wasted away until it became apparent to everyone that she would not live to see the next spring.

The white doctor came—that was Dr. Abbott from Bryson City. He said there was nothing to be done. Molly had one of those strange diseases in which the body feeds upon itself until there is no more; probably it was something disordered in her blood. He didn't know. He tried in his clumsy way to comfort her mother. With nine children, he suggested, Lucille would hardly miss this, the littlest one. But of course Lucille loved Molly best of all.

So she called in her uncle, Coming Back Tuskateeskee, for a consultation. He was a Conjureman, though no longer a very good one—lately the spine seemed to have gone right out of him. He confessed to an apprehension that he was turning blue. "I am like the shadow of a man who lived long ago and cannot quite die," he told Lucille. "I have a man's shape, but not his substance."

The old man stood, hunched over and stick thin, beside the sagging cot in the front room of Reuban's house. "What ails her is Guwangista," he informed Lucille in a voice roughened by alcohol and cigarettes. "This means something is trying to eat something. The trick is finding out what the something is. Guwangista is most frequently caused by birds. We will try to find out if a bird has caused this, and, if so, which bird."

He had grown very methodical of late. There was no longer any part of him that was wild. Tentatively he waved a witch doll fashioned out of wild tobacco and clothed in a scrap of black cloth at his great-niece. She was lying there on one side, knees drawn up toward her shrunken chest like a babe awaiting birth or burial in an urn. He shook long hair the colour of pissed-in snow and hissed, "Listen." He attempted to set the intruding spirit straight. "I am a great ada'wehi! I never fail in anything. I surpass all others."

It wasn't hard, after all, to fool a spirit, he reassured himself. They were just dead things that had once been living, as confused about most things as the rest of us.

"What do you want to bet it's a screech owl's frightened her?" Coming Back asked Molly's mother now. Then, reverting to the ancient formula, "Hah!" He passed the doll over the child's body twice. "I have put it away in the laurel thickets! There I compel it to remain!"

"So you think that's it?" Lucille asked hopefully. She was standing by the cot, hands tangled up in her apron, wringing it like a wet rag. "I thought it might be something like that."

As for Molly lying in her cot, she didn't say anything. Speaking was hard for her at the best of times. For one thing, she scarcely knew how. And, at three years of age, memories fade with the rapidity of dreams; they have as little substance. But there's one thing she did know...and she knew it for a certainty: it weren't the screech owl that done it!

"Better safe than sorry," Coming Back advised his niece, encouraged by her optimism. "Best cover all the bases." He began once more. "Listen! Hah!" And he waved the witch doll at Molly a second time. "It's a hooting owl that's frightened her. At once I have put it away in the spruce thickets. There I compel it to remain. There!" He turned once more to Lucille. "Now, that takes care of screech owls and hooting owls!"

But by this time the spirit of Molly, unbeknownst to her mother and great-uncle, had left her body and was wafting about five feet above it; the beams of the ceiling prevented its further ascent. From this vantage point, she looked down on her shriveled body with a mixture of pity and contempt. It seemed to her as empty and lifeless as the slipped skin of a black timber rattler her brothers had once brought to her invalid's bedside, saying, "Lookit, Molly, what we found us up on the Bald." Yet somehow she was held to that body like a circus balloon that yearns upward at the same time as its ropes hold it fast to its moorings. All in all, she did not find her disembodiment too strange, perhaps because she could not speak. It is often only in the telling that things seem strange to us.

It is not the hoot owl, she tried to tell her great-uncle, but she knew that he could not hear one who spoke with no voice.

"One more thing," Coming Back told Lucille. "There is a chance it could be one of those pesky mountain sprites." A

97

third time he lifted the witch doll high above Molly and spoke with a semblance of authority. "Listen! Ha! I am a great ada'wehi! It is only a mountain sprite that has frightened her. Instantly I have put it away on the bluff! There I compel it to remain!"

He laid the witch doll down on the pillow next to Molly's head. "Well, that about covers it," he told Lucille. "Best I can do. Now, you'll need to blow water on her body just before dark. Do this for four nights, first on the back of the head, next the left shoulder, then the right, and finally...here." He struck his breast with the flat of his hand. "Blow it through a straw. Joe-pye weed'll do. She should be settin' up, facing east." He pulled a dingy brown toque down over his ears, picked up his old duffel coat and a battered paper bag that held a half-empty bottle of Wild Irish Rose. "And, Lucille," he added by way of warning. He shook his finger at her. "Whatever you do, don't take her outside."

"Why not?" asked Lucille.

"The worse thing," Coming Back explained. "A bird might fly overhead, and its shadow fall on her." He shook his head solemnly. "That in itself might be enough to fan the disease right back into her body."

Molly got no better. She got worse. She had visions of herself that were like this: she was an old, old man; she had somehow lived far longer than she should have and so had been consigned alive to a cave not much bigger than a grave. It was a deep cave, and she lay at its very end, at the heart of a high mountain. She could escape if only she could muster the strength to crawl the distance. She could not, of course. She thought she felt the mountain breathe, deeply, as if it slept, and this frightened her. She felt she might be crushed between the ribs of the sleeping mountain.

Since Coming Back had been unable to cure Molly, Lucille saw no help for it but to go to the best conjurewoman on the

Boundary—this was Mama Jesse Black Crow. So she lopped the head off a chicken to have something to pay the old woman, dropped it in Reuban's old hunting-bag, put one of the older girls in charge of the younger ones and started up the old fire road to where Mama Jesse lived—that old woman couldn't be bothered to come down to Cades Cove. She was so rickety her little, bowed legs would scarcely get her across that dirt yard of hers, much less down the mountain and back up again. "So steep going up, a body could stand up straight and bite the ground," folks said about that road. "Going down, you need hobnails in the seat of your pants."

Mama Jesse heard Lucille out, then she told her to go back home and wait for a sign. "It weren't no screech owl, and it weren't no hooting owl neither," she concluded. "No, nor sprite neither. But it's something. That's for sure. And when it comes to you what it is, this is what you do."

She opened her ramshackle cupboard and selected two white beads and a terrapin shell from her stores and handed them to Lucille. She explained the ritual twice and made Lucille repeat it, so she wouldn't forget. Then she added, "Of course the medicine'll have to suit. Coming Back can do that much, can't he?" She hadn't much use for men, especially old men conjurers. She was of the school that held that women will always traffic better with spirits.

Lucille thanked her and offered her the chicken for her trouble. Mama Jesse pointed out that it was on the stringy side. Lucille shrugged. "Take it or leave it," she said, hoping that the old woman would leave it. Of course she didn't, but she didn't eat it either. It came back to partial life and ran around her place for years.

In the linwood forest up around trail's end, Lucille Tuskateeskee Rollover sat on the split carcase of a hemlock tree downed by lightning, her husband's old hunting sack beside her. All around perched mushrooms, feeding silently on the ruined wood like fixed, fungal vultures. On the cusp between winter and spring, the air was cold the same thick way water is; the mist, almost congealed. The woody branches of laurel and rhododendron dripped moisture in icy little tings, making a sound like a leaky pump in winter. Lucille was cold. Her coat wouldn't button all the way—just those two at the top. For the rest, she was too fat or...not fat, she thought. Spread thin. So much life had flowed through her that she had widened, like the capacious delta of a great river. She lifted a hand to her eyes—her fingers were streaked with dried blood from the chicken's neck. Briefly, idly, she poked at some dog hobble with a stick, then some hearts-a-bustin'-with-love, which put her in mind of her mother, Rena Tuskateeskee. Rena had also borne many children. In the end, she took to her bed and refused to leave. Said, "If I do, my uterus'll drop on the floor." Naturally, none of them dared rouse her, lest they have to deal with a runaway womb. So they gave her tea made from the root of hearts-a-bustin'-with-love, which is for falling of the womb, and took what care they could of their Daddy, who was a drinker, and left home as soon as possible.

Lucille left off her poking and sighed and shifted. The log was damp and uncomfortable. Her kneecaps strained against her royal blue polyester trousers; their straining pulled the trousers' waistband too tight and made her stomach ache.

She was just about to stand and be on her way when all of a sudden she heard a crackling in the underbrush. Turning to look over her shoulder, her gaze locked with that of a mangy-looking old she-bear, hunkered down not ten feet away in a patch of bloodred partridgeberry. The bear was staring at her but with a doleful expression, as if she knew Lucille's trouble and deeply sympathized. Lucille was so struck by the sincerity of the bear's expression that she lost all power of movement and simply stared back. After a few moments, the she-bear decorously broke eye contact and turned, but in a leisurely fashion, loping lopsidedly away. As Lucille watched her shimmer like vapour off concrete on a hot day, then waver into particles before dissolving into the greenwood, it occurred to her that this was the spirit of the very bear whose fat she had cut up and boiled for oil going on four years ago.

Four years ago.... At the time, Molly was no bigger than the coil on a lady slipper, than a crooked finger, and she's bobbing up and down in Lucille's womb like a lure on a fishhook, waiting for something to happen, for life to befall her.

In the meantime, Lucille's setting up at the table in the front room, three months gone with child (Molly, that is) and singing to herself, a sort of low, twanging sound like the one string of a washboard bass: Wahhhh! She's cutting up the fat off the old she-bear that had lived in a cage down next to the Dairy Queen. After a long time of waiting to be free, this bear had finally died of despair , and Lucille, being appraised of this, had claimed the corpse. When she's done cutting, she'll boil the strips for bear oil. That's good for earaches and bad chests too—all winter long, coughs rattled around in her kids like bats in caves.

But then she spies through the window Reuban. He's coming through the linwood, dragging that damned, bloody sack behind him. A big heap of a man, like a whole pile of logs moving on two legs, and his face all puffy and splotched with dark. Lucille lays down her knife, then picks it up again, and stands with the sharp tip of the blade pointed up. Alert.

But Reuban doesn't come inside just yet. He stops by the stump and, bending stiffly, lays down the bag.

Lucille crosses to the door and walks out onto the porch. The torn screen door bangs shut behind her. "You shoot 'em?" she calls over to her husband.

"'Course I shot 'em!" Reuban snarls. "What else would I do?"

"Oh, Reuban, you could've snared 'em," she complains, dropping down the porch steps. "Everybody else does!"

"And lose one foot in the snare?" Reuban demands.

"Well, then we could eat 'em at least," says Lucille, shaking her head. Walking over to the stump, she prods the blood-stained sack with her big toe. "I can't for the life of me grasp why you have to blow them all to Kingdom Come!"

"I like blowin' them to Kingdom Come," Reuban points out. He throws open the bag and pulls out a limp, mangled rabbit with its head blown half off and lays him onto the stump. Then, reaching down, he picks up the old, blood-stained hatchet propped up against the stump and whacks off first one foot, then the other. "Get a fire going under that dyepot," he orders her, tossing the despoiled rabbit aside and reaching into the bag for another.

(For a while there, just after he got loose from the pen, he was into shooting rabbits and dying their feet green or pink or purple and fixing them up with a mounting and a chain before selling them to Trader Tom to sell for goodluck charms.)

Then he suddenly barks, "Do you hear me, woman?" And, wheeling around, he strikes her hard across the face. And before she knows it, she's down on her hands and knees in the dirt, and he's beating on her like she was a drum, but with hard chops of his hand, and she's crying and screaming and calling out, "Why? Why are you hitting me, Reuban? What have I done?" And he's yelling, "You went with another man while I was locked up in that pen. You bitch! I ought to kill you!"

Without thinking any further, just doing, Lucille reached deep into the hunting-sack, still sticky with the chicken's blood, and ran her hand along the seam at its bottom. A second later, she pulled out one bedraggled, bloodsoaked rabbit's foot.

Following Mama Jesse's instructions, although grudgingly, Coming Back brewed a tea made from an herb called rabbit's tail to blow over Molly's body and a decoction of another herb called rabbit tobacco or life everlasting to blow down her throat through joe-pye-weed stem, and he recited the formula for rabbits—for Lucille had known the moment she pulled that severed foot from the bag that it was Reuban's slaughtering rabbits that had brought this illness upon their little daughter: "It is only a rabbit that has frightened her," rasped Coming Back. "Instantly I have put it away on a mountain ridge. There in the broom sage I compel it to remain!" And he raised the witch doll high above Molly with a palsied hand.

As for Lucille, she made atonement to the offended rabbits this way: carrying tiny Molly in her arms, she climbed Gregory Bald, below which the rabbits are known to have their council house. She placed the sick child on a white blanket and laid the terrapin shell that Mama Jesse had given her on the ground. While the five spirits listened, she spoke to each of them—to Red Dog in the Sun Land and Blue Dog in the Frigid Land and Black Dog in the Darkening Land and White Dog in Wahala—as Mama Jesse had coached her to, concluding with, "On Wahala you repose, White Terrapin. Now you have swiftly drawn near to hearken. It is for you to loosen its hold on the bone. Relief is accomplished!"

In the terrapin's shell, she placed two white beads together with a little rabbit's ear that she had carried there in an old baby food jar. Then, standing and lifting Molly up in her arms, she cursed Reuban Rollover, because the varicose veins that wound around her thick legs were beating like drums and writhing like live wires or snakes. "Goddam you, Reuban Rollover!" she cried. "Goddam you!"

Later that same spring, Lucille sat at the table, fitting newsprint into shoes that had holes in them but would have to last another season. It was raining, a soft, persistent misting that seemed to exude from the earth rather than fall upon it— the forest was bathed with it as with a gentle perspiration.

As for Molly, she lay propped up in bed, weak but getting better as time passed. A few days before, she had asked her mother to move the bed so that she could look out the window to the patch of yard between the porch and the forest, and, since then, as long as it was light, she had sat there, staring and staring.

"Molly," Lucille asked. "What is it you're looking at out there?"

"Oh," said Molly offhandedly. "I'm looking at all the rabbits, Mama."

"The rabbits?" Lucille asked, her voice rising sharply on the last word. Her heart turned over in her breast like a baby in the womb. Her hand leapt to her throat, circling her windpipe, making her catch her breath. Rising, she crossed quickly to Molly's bed. Placing her hand on the bedhead, she leaned forward and peered out the window to where Molly was looking .

Dozens of them. All around the edge of the wood, their outlines rendered soft and indistinct by the shadows thrown by the trees and the silvery green mist. Silent, alert, poised on their hind legs. Ready for flight. Their frail defensiveness so like that of women, Lucille realized, who, lacking strength, must also protect themselves with vigilant alertness. And she understood from the way they held themselves that they had come from curiosity but also to offer their protection to one whom they had almost destroyed. And behind them, almost invisible in the dark woods, the bluish, vaporous shadow spirit of the bear who had died of despair, whose heartbeat she felt rock her own breast, so much did the two of them seem to resonate in time.

The Raven Mocker

I'm just a poor, wayfarin' stranger,
a-passin' through this world of woe.

The three old men huddled together at the front of the
Cherokee High School gymnasium; they bent over their
guitars like they were praying over bodies prostrate with
illness and picked at their steel strings in that methodical,
half-expectant way women squeeze lice from a child's head,
listening with ears cocked for the snap and the ping. They
were painfully aware—as one is of a burn—of a particular

woman: gnarled as a wind-stunted tree, she sat half-hunkered down and hunched over in the front row of mourners.

And there's no sickness, toil or danger
In that fair land to which I go!

Knowing that she had come, that she was here, the old men felt their hearts rattle in their chests, like loose coughs.

I'm going there to meet my mother!
I'm going there no more to roam!

The old shape-note spiritual they sang inched out close-harmonied, a hoecake of dense sound, flat, packed tight with chords and darkly resonant. The gym's occupants could scarcely make out the words, lodged far up the old men's noses and reverberating there, above the thump and whine of the guitars, across the softly shining expanses of blond wood divided and subdivided into ritual spaces and liminal zones by the broad strokes of red and blue and green—the basketball court—and the high floating arch of the beamed and girdered underbelly of the school's copper roof. But the tune scraped at the memories of the mourners, and performed in this spun-out, flattened way, the song took on the aspect of keening, low and haltingly rhythmic, like the slow beating of a head against the wall, the substitution of sound for pain. Reassuring. We are Christians here, the mourners directed their thoughts at the woman: they knew she possessed organs of hearing other than her ears. Your magic cannot touch us.

That's what you think....

The mourners wore tank tops and T-shirts, shapeless shifts, blue jeans and shorts. Children wandered aimlessly about half naked and shoeless in the close July heat. Two little girls seated in front of the big pewter coffin under the basketball hoop squabbled loudly and relentlessly over a battered

Country Western Barbie. Cherokee mourn with apparent casualness—not with the stiff formality of white men.

And all the while, whispers like wind through tall, dry grass:

"Do you see who's here?"

"I never thought they'd be letting her out!"

Christians or no Christians, there were those among them who had heard the harsh croak of the raven as it prepares to dive, who had seen the night-goer fly in a shape of fire against a sky filled with shadow.

I'm just a-going over Jordan.

(Tsusgina'i! The ghost country!)

I'm just a-going over home.

(Usunhiyi! The dark land!)

"It ain't right, Wally," the woman who was the object of all this fearful interest observed in a hissed aside to her husband. Liza Light-Up-The-Sky Talahawa Barkman was her name. She was the corpse's eldest daughter. "Mama's face is directly under that basketball hoop!" Liza complained. Forty-eight this spring, she looked closer to 80—it wasn't a natural thing; it was because of the extra years she had added to her own through her unspeakable activities. Her complexion, once as red and smooth as clay and a source of great pride to her, had taken on a greenish cast, like bronze when it tarnishes; she was wrinkled up one side and down the other, like a piece of paper that's been crumpled every which way and then flattened out again; and her hair was as blind-eye grey as pewter and as dull; she wore it pulled back into a sparse ponytail so tight that it made her eyes, red-brown as a fox's, start from her head. "What could Quatie have been thinking?" she asked her husband.

(Good God, Quatie, it's Liza! Liza's here! The corpse in the coffin recognized her elder daughter's voice and now communicated her alarm to her second daughter Quatie—Quatie and she had always subscribed to the same wavelength. For Ivy Light-Up-The-Sky, who had died Tuesday, was still in her body; she was as yet unburied; and consciousness dissipates slowly. Like foam washed up on a beach, it lingers, caught on the rocks like lace torn on jagged fingernails.

It's all right, Mother, thought Quatie—she was the fat woman in the faded red bandanna seated on a folding chair to one side of the coffin. I'm keeping an eye on her.)

"Anybody want to play basketball?" Liza cried out in a loud voice. "Anybody want to score a point right onto Mama's face? Go on! It don't matter. She's dead."

Quatie actively ignored her: she didn't so much as look in her direction, although she was aware of her in every cell of her body. She just wants closer, but she's not getting closer, thought Quatie, folding her arms across her chest, as if to shield her own heart from one who might seek to take the years left to her.

It was the truth. Liza did want closer. Just that little bit. She wanted closer to see her Mama's face. She hadn't seen her Mama's face in so long. Six long years. "Somebody, move that coffin out from under that hoop and over this a-way a little!" she demanded, but nobody so much as looked in her direction; it was as if she hadn't spoken. Angry, she shrunk up all bitty, like a slug you sprinkled salt on. She glared at Quatie, wrinkling up her hawk nose. "Woman like a snake in the tall grass, rattling a warning," she hissed.

"Now, now, be good," Wally reminded her helplessly. "It's a sad day. It's your mother's gone, Liza."

"No," Liza corrected him. She sniffed the air speculatively, like a dog downwind. "No, she's here somewhere." And she peered sharply around as if her gaze was a sharp tool with which she might sever Ivy's ghost self from the protective shadows in which it lingered.

The matter-of-factness with which she spoke, the bold confidence of her glance, made Wally's pink bald head mist with sweat, and his chest expand like an accordian. How could he have slept with her in the crook of his arm and her hand upon his chest, the palm flat, the fingers curled just slightly, the nails dug lightly in, for those years? She had been his sweetheart. He was lucky to be alive!

To one side of the coffin stood a floral tribute that read, in pink and white carnations, GRANNY. To the other stood a telephone composed of purple mums with the legend JESUS CALLED.

"Jesus! In a pig's eye!" Liza snorted, seeing this. "Jesus called? What'd he say, Mama? Time's up?" she cried.

Back aways, when Liza was crazy with wanting a child and her first husband Ronnie Talahawa couldn't get one on her, she had prayed to Jesus—oh, how she had prayed, and she had made offerings to him in special, secret places, of white beads in terrapin shells and featherfew: please, whatever I have done.... Only God knows where Jesus had been at the time, for there had been no children for Liza—no children ever. So Liza had her a bone to pick with Mr. Jesus.

"Liza!" Wally warned her. He was a Born Again Christian. And again. And again. He was prone to lapses, and when he came back to Christ, well, it was all right because He was always right where he had left Him—in the liquor cabinet. Gleaming, amber, liquid. "If you don't mind your mouth, you'll go straight to Hell."

"And where else would I be going the way things are stacking up?" Liza challenged him. Wally had to concede she had a point.

The old men coughed and hawked and spat and sung:

I feel my sins are all forgiven!
My hopes are stayed on things above!
I'm going away to you, bright Heaven!
Where all is peace and joy and love!

I'm going there to meet my mother!
I'm going there no more to roam.

"You'd better believe it, Brothers and Sisters! You'd better believe you're going there no more to roam!" a powerful, adenoidal voice cut short the refrain. "Believe! Believe!" It was Reverend Josiah Etowah, who was making a slow progress through the crowd toward the coffin, shaking hands and slapping backs and tousling the hair of the children who littered his path. "Ivy Light-Up-the-Sky is one good Christian woman that ain't never going to do no more roaming! No! She's going straight to Paradise, God willing, and we're here, brothers and sisters, to send her on her way! Ain't we, Sister Quatie? We're here to recommend our sister Ivy to the Good Lord. Ain't that so, ladies and gentlemen?"

Josiah began his eulogy of Ivy with a list of her virtues but soon wandered off into the more rugged terrain of Hell. Finally, the terrified screams of children stopped him short. "That's enough!" he conceded. "You know the rest." Then he invited people up to have their last look at Ivy before the coffin was closed.

As the people filed by, Liza gnashed her teeth and made low growling sounds in her throat like a dog. She shifted restlessly this way and that way; she wriggled like a snake trying to shed its itchy old skin. She remembered her dreams—how they had turned dark with age; how she ached with them now, like they were soft teeth. Ivy was to blame...and Quatie, her sister. Liza was certain that, in the early days of Ronnie and her courtship, the two of them had cast a plug of tobacco into the fire and called on the Blue Hawk to alight between her and him; that they had evoked the Blue Hawk in order to separate her and her man so that Quatie could have him for herself. Liza had been the pretty one, after all. It was Quatie who would have to resort to conjuring to get a man. And Quatie had a hankering for Ronnie. Quite a hankering. Don't think Liza didn't know it!

Yu! On high you repose, O Blue Hawk, there at the far distant lake. The tobacco has come to be your recompense. Now you have arisen at once and come down. You have alighted midway between them where they two are standing.

"Quatie Light-Up-The-Sky! You wanted my Ronnie!" Liza exploded, half-starting from her seat, but prevented from leaving it entirely by the handcuffs that bound her to the back of Wally's chair. Everyone turned to look at her, startled by the sudden clamour.

"Make a scene, and you're out of here," Wally reminded her. He was right, too. A man was waiting who would take her away. And a car. Grudgingly, Liza settled back in her seat.

Quatie had wanted Ronnie. Liza was right about that. But nothing could have stopped Liza from marrying him, not all their begging her please not to, not all their conniving or their conjuring. Or so she had thought.

But it was a slow spell the two women had cast, and, like many spells which only half take, it killed what it was meant to secure. In the end, Ronnie lay dead in the Cherokee Hospital with a liver so full of holes you could have strained crabapple jelly through it. It was the moonshine from up around Newfound Gap that done it. Like drinking liquid fiberglass, the white doctor had said: ten years of that would kill anybody.

So the Blue Hawk did alight midway between them at last, and all the children that might have been born to them, but for the quickening that never happened, died slow deaths within Liza's womb. 'Course Ronnie swore up and down that it weren't so, that she was so barren trying to get a child on her was like trying to plow a salt lick into a cornfield. But Liza knew he was wrong. She had life in her. Why, there was a whole mess of people milling around inside her groin. She could feel them all squeezed in there...they had scarcely room to move. And at night they'd talk to her, only not so's anybody could listen. They'd say, "Mother, let us out!" But Ronnie's seed couldn't turn the key; couldn't unlock the prison of her womb and usher all those formless souls into The Light—his seed had been spoiled by the conjuring. So the years went by, and every night those babies who might have been her sons and daughters would plead with her, "We're growing old, Mother! Please, oh, please, let us out before we die!" And finally they had begun to die, one by one. The pleading voices grew quieter and fewer and eventually ceased, and the womb she bore around inside of her, once swollen and heavy with what might have been, grew light and as empty as a blown seed pod.

Liza fainted. Slumped forward and half slid off her chair. When she came to, it was with the heavy sensation that time had jumped ahead, leaving her straddled somewhere in the past.

"You all right?" Wally was asking her. His voice seemed to come from a great distance.

"It's close in here."

"It's a hot day."

"If you ask me, she needs some air." Onlookers offered their opinions.

"I want to see my Mama's face once last time." Liza, though fuddled, saw her opportunity and took it.

Everyone turned to Quatie. She hesitated for the length of a heart's beat. Then she shook her head. No.

Liza settled back in her seat. Tears as sharp as a handful of nettles stung her withered cheeks, as she watched the mourners file by the coffin in a shambling, leisurely line. Suddenly she sat up straight.

A little girl had come to the head of the line. Small for her six years, she had legs so spindly it didn't seem likely that they could hold her up for long—that was because she had been a twin, born months before her time. Unlike most of the other children at the funeral, she was almost painfully dressed up in a starchy blue dress, white anklets trimmed with machine lace, and shining black patent leather Mary Jane shoes. She stood on tiptoes and peered into the coffin. Then she suddenly struck at the corpse with her hand and screamed, "Big Granny! Big Granny! Oh, get up, Big Granny! Get up and walk!"

"Wenona?" Liza exhaled sharply. Wenona was her great-niece, Quatie's grand-daughter, but Liza had not seen her since she was a baby.

Quatie stepped forward and pulled the hysterical child to her, letting her bury her face in her ample stomach. Over her head, she met Liza's gaze and held it.

Back off, Liza, thought Quatie. Just back off.

Like many plain women who despair of getting a husband when they are young, Quatie needn't have fussed. After a spell she married Matty Stinger to whom she bore seven children. The youngest of these was Roselle.

When Roselle turned thirteen, she complained of a severe stomach ache. Twenty hours later, her grandmother Ivy pulled two of the tiniest little girls anybody had ever seen still breathing from the child's womb with the long-handled wooden spoons the old woman used for beanbread.

Nobody could explain either the pregnancy or how anyone had failed to notice it, apart from the fact that Roselle had always been heavy. For her part, Roselle swore up and down that no man had ever touched her in that way, and she stuck by her story. She would have nothing to do with the inexplicable twins, but returned to her jacks games and jump ropes as soon as she could, leaving her mother and grandmother to name the babies—Wenona and Ramona—and to tend them like they were sick puppies.

The two women, mothers fifteen times over, set the card-board box the twins slept in close by the fire and dangled rags dipped in sugar syrup for them to suck on and poured as much star grass root tea as they could make down them—they were two colicky babies, always doubled up in pain and yelling because, when they had been born, their insides weren't half finished.

One day when Wenona and Ramona were about sitting-up and falling-over age, Liza paid a call. She had been married to Walter Barkman going on two years then and was sitting real pretty by Cherokee standards. No log cabin for her, but a brand new ranchstyle home with three bedrooms and a washer and dryer right on the premises. The Oconaluftee Joke and Rock Shop and the adjoining laudromat and photo-finish kiosk had done so well in season that once a year for three years running he had taken Liza to Disney World in Florida and bought her all kinds of souvenirs. They had TV trays that said Disney World and a whole set of patio glasses and beach towels. Not like her first husband Ronnie Talahawa, who hadn't owned the land he squatted on, much less the shirt on his back. Liza was still beautiful then—dark complexioned women hold onto their beauty longer than fair ones—and she stood tall and straight, not bent like now, and her hair was black and shiny and long.

"I respect as how you've brought these babies along," Liza began. "Tell you the truth, I didn't think they would make it through that first week. I never did see anything so little in all my born days."

"I seen things littler," said Ivy, but Ivy was a midwife, and she prided herself on the breadth of her experience. And she also liked having that last word. "I seen babies the size of your thumb," she added, hooking her thumb at Liza. She had never had a lot of use for her eldest daughter, even less now that she was always going on about Disney World.

"Well, I sure haven't," concluded Liza, deliberately not rising to her mother's bait. "Anyways you done a fine job. Only I was thinking...how many of you is there living here? There's Mama and you and Matty Stinger and Roselle and Audrey and June Lily (they were Quatie's three children that were still at home) and now there's these two babies...."

"We get by," Quatie interrupted her.

"It's a two-room cabin, Quatie," Liza pointed out.

"We get by," Quatie repeated.

"That's eight people!"

"We get by. How many times do I have to say it?" Quatie asked.

"When you'uns were growing up, and Annie and her husband were building their place up Deep Creek there was eleven people living in this cabin," Ivy recollected.

"Point is, Mama, I live in a three-bedroom, ranchstyle home with a washer and dryer." Liza was sitting on the edge of the old twig chair now, tugging at her fingers like they were gloves that she had tried and tried to pull off but couldn't manage to somehow. She was always pulling at herself like her flesh was a torment to her. "And you know how I always did want children of my own and never could have them. You have enough on your hands without these two babies." She spoke all in a rush. "Hell! Between you, you've had all the babies anybody could ever want! Give them to me and Wally. Oh, please. They'll have a good life, better than you can give them." She stopped then and looked quickly away and then down at her lap, because she more than half expected them to say "no," and now she'd probably offended them. However, much to her surprise, Ivy hesitated only a moment before saying, "We'll think us on it."

"Mama!" exclaimed Quatie indignantly.

"Quatie, I said we'd think us on it," Ivy told her firmly.

Now who knows what was on Ivy's mind when she told Liza that. Maybe the rheumatism in her hip was acting up, what with all the wet weather they'd been having that spring, and the chasing around after babies was getting her down. Or maybe she just wanted to string Liza along. The old woman was known for her high-handedness; she'd sooner leave you that little bit of slack and then pull you up short than deal straight with you. Because where was the power in straight dealing? She was the matriarch of the Light-Up-the-Sky family, after all, the old one, the one in charge, and she had to have ways of keeping folks off balance and in line so everything would work right.

In any case, Liza got herself all worked up. She should have known better—even Wally told her to slow down; she knew how Ivy operated—but Liza had wanted babies for so long that she couldn't contain herself.

She went to Sears and bought two matching cribs with a drawing of Winnie the Pooh holding balloons on strings on them and a padded, vinyl-covered changing table, and bags of Huggies on special, and one of those deodorized diaper pails....

And every time she bought something new, she'd go up to Ivy's cabin and set herself down for a cup of Lady Slipper Tea, because her nerves were shot and always had been, and she'd say, "I just got the cutest chest of drawers. It's got bunnies all over it," and then she'd ask, "When can I take the babies home?"

And Ivy would wait a moment—that was her style, not to reply immediately, to make her interlocutor wait—and then as casual as you please but in a tone that utterly forbade any further discussion, "I haven't said you could have those girls, Liza. Now have I? I said we'd think us on it."

Until Liza was ready to pull her hair out. And this went on for months and months, until finally spring passed into summer, and the damp lifted enough for the dull ache in Ivy's hip that was like an animal gnawing there with slow teeth to ease a bit, and Liza come up the hill to tell her mother and sister that she had just bought the girls matching walkers.

It was then that Ivy said as cool as can be, her back to Liza as she was fixing tea, "You can't have 'em."

"What?" asked Liza.

"I said, you can't have 'em," repeated Ivy.

"But...why not?" cried Liza.

"It don't suit us," said Ivy. And that was all she would ever say about the matter.

"Wenona!" Liza called now to the little girl held tight in her grandmother's embrace before the coffin. "Wenona! It's me! It's Liza Light-Up-the-Sky! It's your Mama!"

Wenona stared at the strangely crabbed woman manacled to the chair. Her eyes widened until the whites were visible around the pupils. She had heard the story, of course; it was the kind of story told alongside the woodstove on a dark winter's night while a shrieking wind wound the cabin around with swirling veils of snow, "Did you know...." and Big Granny would break in, "Hush, now, Roselle. She'll keep us up all night with her terrors if you don't."

And now suddenly the night-goer had returned from the Spirit World, the creature whose face she had seen glow in the ashes of wood tormented by fire, whose proud, slim body and elegant hands she had seen in her dreams from a time before she had words—this same beautiful woman, this bearer of gifts, had grown strangely misshapen with the passage, but something about her was still recognizable to Wenona. Her smell of blood.

The child opened her mouth and began to scream, an unnatural scream, a high pitched siren's wail that went on and on and seemed almost mechanical, divorced from terror. She had been screaming that scream inside of herself for the past six years.

"Stop it, Wennie," Quatie ordered her. She shook her firmly. "Leave off, Liza," she hollered at her sister. "The child's given to terrors, and no wonder with what she seen!"

"Wenona! Wenona! I'm your real mama!" cried Liza.

"Liza, stop this!" Wally begged her. "Please! Not now!"

"But I am! She is! She's my daughter! She has to know I am her mother!"

"Get her out of here" Quatie insisted. "Somebody get her out of here." Wenona had not stopped screaming. "Wenona, stop that." Quatie struck the girl hard across the face.

That was when the man dropped his cigarette to the floor, extinguishing it with a quick grind of his heel, and stepped forward. Ben was his name. He was a white man, over six feet tall and very strong. All this time he had never been far away, and, except for now and again when things were quiet and he had retired to the hallway for a smoke, he had been watching the patient in his charge. Now, as Quatie proved unable to silence Wenona and was yelling out for the love of God who was a man around here and going to help her, and people were stirring and even standing up, and women were saying to their men, "Go on! Help her," and men, uneasy, were grunting and shuffling and looking for all the world like they were about to do something when in fact they were only stalling, hoping some other man would do it first, and a few children had begun to whimper and others to scream, then Ben hitched up his pants and began to elbow it through the crowd to where Liza was rattling her manacles and banging her seat up and down against the shining floor and shrieking to Wenona that yes, she was her mother, that yes, it was time she knew that. "That's why I ate your sister's heart!" she cried.

At this Wenona burst into even louder, even more high-pitched screams—she sounded like a stuck pig. She went stiff as a board, and began to shake all over, like a washing-machine in the rinse cycle.

Too bad, Liza, thought Ben, shaking his head. And you wanted to come so bad. You talked of nothing else.

"Liza," he murmured, bending over her. "You're being bad now, Liza, and that means we gotta go back." Squatting down behind her, he unlocked her handcuffs.

The moment she felt the pressure on her wrists ease, she sprang forward, knocking the chair over and topping Ben backwards. Then she darted toward the coffin, half leaping, half stumbling and scrambling over chairs and people.

At the sight of her, terrorized women leapt to their feet, screamed and clutched their children to them. Quatie seized Wenona and dragged her, still shrieking and rigid behind the coffin.

Then, just as Liza reached the bare, shining floor of the gymnasium and started across it, a sound came from within the coffin, a horrible sound, a sound like nobody had ever heard before in their lives, human but inhuman too, like an echo of a scream heard from far away and possibly from long ago.

Liza stopped dead in her tracks, and a moment later she was lying at the bottom of a pile of teenage boys with two broken ribs—Coach Bob Duck had given the signal, and the quarterback of Cherokee Braves had brought her down with a flying tackle, followed by most of his teammates.

In the silence that followed, somebody said—and everyone heard—"O Sweet Jesus who is my Saviour...Was that Ivy?"

"This is the story, Wenona. It's a terrible story. The story of your sister Ramona that was your twin and looked just like you and was killed by a terrible Raven Mocker." The chair by the woodstove creaked in protest as the young woman lowered her bulk into its rush seat. It was dark outside. The wind whined an aimless tune, like a crazy person humming. She spun her song round and round the isolated cabin, like she was wrapping it up. Gu ti ha. It is snowing. Go la. Winter.

"What's a Raven Mocker?" Wenona asked. She squatted before the woodstove, her hands on her knees for balance.

"A Raven Mocker is the worst kind of witch there is," Roselle informed her. "When somebody is real sick, so sick that she might even die, here comes the Raven Mocker, only you can't see her, because she's invisible, and besides, it's probably dark outside." Roselle looked over her shoulder to the room's single window. The dark stared back at her with its black eye. "Like it is tonight," she said. "And the Raven Mocker stands outside the house, and she worries that sick person. She stamps on the roof, and she beats on the side of the house, and she scrapes branches across the windowpanes. Just torments her. And unless there is a even more powerful conjure woman than her inside that house, she can even force her way in. When she does that, she lifts up the sick person from the bed and throws her down again...just to rattle her up good, and sometimes she even drags her out to the floor. Because all that fires the sickness. Makes the person die faster."

"Why does she want the person to die?" Wenona wanted to know. Her eyes, fixed on Roselle, were wide with terror.

"So she can eat her heart," Roselle told her. "When a Raven Mocker eats a person's heart, she eats all the years she might have lived if she hadn't worried her to death. That's how you can tell if someone is a Raven Mocker. They look older than they should. It's on account of all those years they've eaten—the years add up after a while."

"Why do they call her a Raven Mocker?" Wenona asked.

"Because she flies at night in the shape of a fiery cross," Roselle told her, spreading her arms out wide. "And just before she dives, she makes this harsh, croaking sound, like a raven makes before it dives." Roselle dropped her hands to her knees and leaned forward. "So, you listen out, Wenona, and, if you ever hear such a terrible sound as that, you run you for cover."

Wenona shuddered. She didn't want to, but she couldn't resist. "Tell me about my sister," she whispered.

Roselle leaned back against the chair. "Well, you were just babies then," she said. "About a year old, I reckon. It was night-time, winter-time. Ramona had the croup. Of the two of you, she was always the sickliest. And she was coughing away. And Mama and Big Granny Ivy, they were taking turns getting up with her, but pretty much everybody else was asleep." Roselle paused. She looked to either side, then leaned toward Wenona and spoke in a voice lowered to a whisper. "When, all of a sudden, Mama's sister Liza walks in, and she goes to where Ramona's lying there, coughing, and she picks her up and looks at her. By this time Mama's awake, and she says...."

"'What are you doing here? Liza?'" Wenona took up the tale. She had heard it so often.

"That's right," said Roselle. "And Liza says, as cool as can be, 'I know what happened now, with Roselle, I mean.' And Mama says...."

"'What do you mean, what happened?'" Wenona supplied.

Roselle continued. "And Liza said, 'These were my babies Roselle had. My babies that had waited so long to be born and that just couldn't on account of that spell you and Mama laid on me and Ronnie. So what happened was, they ended up in Roselle's body by mistake.' And Mama asked..."

"'What are you talking about?'" said Wenona.

"And Liza said, 'I've thought it through, and I know I'm right. Wenona and Ramona are my babies. They just got put in Roselle by mistake. 'Cause there was nowhere else for them to go. Now, I'm going to take them back.' And Mama said...."

"'They were born of Roselle,'" related Wenona.

"Right," said Roselle. "She said, 'Your body ain't had nothing to do with these babies, Liza. Now you put that child down. Can't you see you're worriting it?'because Ramona was yelling her head off by this time, Liza had such a strange, twisted up expression on her face, and you were too, standing up in your bed and just screeching. But just as Mama started toward Liza, Liza pulled out this long knife, and she didn't even hesitate. She just stuck it into Ramona's chest and yanked and pulled at it until she up and flipped out her heart. Oh, Lordy! There was blood everywhere. And then...then she pushed the mess into her mouth. I've never seen anything so horrible. Nobody could move. Nobody could even take in what had happened. And she chewed and chewed and finally she swallowed. She was all over with blood. Blood was in her hair. Her hands. It was all over her face. And after a minute, she took a deep breath, and then she said, 'If I eat their hearts, then this time they can be reborn through me. I have a new husband now, and his seed will unlock the door'...whatever that means! And she turned to reach for you." Roselle reached out and took Wenona by the collar and pulled her toward her. Wenona gasped in fright. "And you!" laughed Roselle. "You let out a shriek like I've never heard this side of a hog sticking, and Big Granny Ivy, who had snuck up behind her by this time, hit her over the head with the skillet for making cornbread in, and she was screaming too. Anyway, that was the last anybody ever seen of that Raven Mocker, because they took her away shortly afterwards, and they locked her, and they thrown away the key."

Wenona settled back onto her haunches and stared reflectively at the flames waving at her through the grate of the woodstove.

"Roselle," she asked after a moment. "Do you think it's true that we were the Raven Mocker's true daughters, just born out of your body?"

Roselle shrugged. "Who knows?" she said, standing in all her enormity. "I 'spect so. I myself had nothing to do with you. That's the onliest thing I know for sure."

Wenona nodded. A sad, shrivelled child who looked suddenly, by the light of the dancing fire, far older than her six years. She turned away from her natural mother to meet the night's cold stare, and for a time she crouched where it was warm and listened to the wind sing its crazy song:

I'm going there to meet my mother.
I'm going there no more to roam.
I'm just a-going over Jordan.
I'm just a-going over home.

Ghost Teachers

There is a peak within the Boundary, which white men call
Rattlesnake Knob but the Elders call Atsilawai, Fire's
Relative. This mountain, which is in Swain County, lies to the
east of the Oconaluftee River and two miles northeast of
Yellow Hill. A group of Cherokee once observed a ball of fire
fly through the air from this summit toward Highlands over
in Macon County—that is where the mountain got its Indian
name. Folks reckoned the ball of fire to be an ulunsuti, the
wondrous crystal. Conjecture was that the crystal's human
owner had hidden it on the remote mountain top to guard it

against thieves, for ulunsutis are rare and convey upon their owners great power. Perhaps the owner of the crystal had died, and the ulunsuti was going forth from its hiding place in search of him. Ulunsutis are like dogs in this respect: this is the sort of thing they are likely to do. It was probably hungry as well. An ulunsuti needs blood on a regular basis.

Where the name Rattlesnake Knob came from was this: a white man climbing the mountain one day was bitten by a big rattlesnake. He did not die, however, or even fall ill. As luck would have it, he was not wearing wooden clogs, the typical footwear of most of the white inhabitants of the region, but leather boots he had bought new that day from a pedlar from Down Yonder.

A place can be magic. Sometimes it is magic because it is the place where magic things are, and sometimes it's the other way around. Sometimes, too, magic simply erupts and consumes everything in sight, like a fire—the flame is cool, invisible; the fire burns slow; we cannot see it, but in our hearts we hear it hiss and lick.

No doubt about it: there are points of convergence, openings between worlds, spaces a soul can slip between and squeeze through the other side. There is energy and a constant vibration like a silvery humming—this lies below the crust of silence that forms over molten madness. There is a hunger on the part of what has died to walk once more with the living. Trees have spirits and fragments of human souls hang torn from their branches—these souls fly through the forests like panicked birds before a fire. The dead are all around us in bits and pieces. A little known fact: spirits dissolve more quickly than styrofoam but more slowly than ever we imagined.

The burying ground was just this side of Birdtown. Turn off the highway to Bryson onto that gravel road just after the Thrifty Motel and head up mountain.... It only takes five or ten minutes to get there from the highway. The road's pretty good up until the end when it becomes badly rutted. A lot of comings and goings since they laid old John Paint to rest there back in 1956, a lot of startings and stoppings of automobiles and backings up of pickup trucks and quick reverses—John Paint's was the first body buried in this particular graveyard, which is known locally as The New Burying Ground, it being as good a name as any. Not much to look at in and of itself. Crabgrass. A few beleaguered pines, which the wind has twisted into shapes like dancers who bend and twirl. Fifteen graves, scattered helter skelter over the bald—the bald is rocky outcrop and you dig where you can. Some of the graves are marked with crosses made by nailing two boards together, the names crookedly burnt into the wood; plasticized cards in metal holders stuck into the ground identify others: Moses Stickhorse, drove off a cliff, aged eighteen; Glorianne Peacock, 1901-1979, beloved wife of Harry Peacock, also, at one time, George Saunders and Amos Fox. She outlived them all. Some of the cards boast photographs; others are so weathered and clay-bespattered that they are practically illegible. And the graves are of varying sizes—the Cherokee bury miscarried babies, which accounts for the large number of tiny graves and legends like Baby Stinger, born and died in the summer of 1963, age 0. The graves in the New Burying Ground did have one thing in common, however: they all looked west and, looking west off the bald, you could see clear into tomorrow. Blue mountains that go on forever and never stop. A window onto an eternity the cool colour of smoke.

Lucille Rollover stood beside Mama Jesse Black Crow's newly dug grave. At a signal from the preacher, Josiah Etowah, who stood a little back and to her right, she hitched up her chin and began to sing:

Down in some green valley in a lonesome place,
where the wind it does whistle, the notes to increase,
I'd think of Pretty Saro, whose waist is so neat,
And knows no better pastime than to be with my sweet.

Lucille's voice was high-pitched and nasal; her delivery flat and expressionless—this was the style in which these old mountain ballads are traditionally sung.

My love, he longs for her and I understand.
He wants a rich maiden with house and with land.
I'm only a poor girl. I've not silver nor gold.
I've none of the fine things that a rich girl should hold.

Pretty Saro, thought Talahina Bluebird, who stood just downgrave of Lucille.... Her mind revved like the engine of a sportscar. A love ballad in a minor key. Not a spiritual. No Amazing Grace, how sweet the sound. No Sometimes I feel like a motherless child. No mention of God or Jesus or that old time religion.... Well, she reflected, the woman they were burying today had had no use for spirituals. What was it she was reported to have told Ivy Light Up the Sky when the old Granny woman had tried to lure her to church up in Yellow Hill? "Ivy, I have outlived Christianity the way I have outlived grief."

I wish I were a blackbird with a heart full of song.
I'd sing to Miss Saro all about a great wrong.

I wish I had known Mama Jesse Black Crow, thought Talahina Bluebird.

I'd sing it by the grey dam where the waters o'er flow,
and I'd beg Pretty Saro to let my love go.

And if Pretty Saro didn't let the singer's beloved go, Talahina thought, Mama Jesse Black Crow would have probably lain a curse upon her and she would have dropped dead in her traces. Mama Jesse had been a famous conjure woman, most prized for curses directed against faithless lovers. She travelled, when she ventured abroad into the world below her isolated mountain home on Rattlesnake Knob, in the shape of a black crow and had not died so much...this was the speculation...as shed her ancient body. How else to explain the peculiar condition in which the Cherokee police, Ira Bushyhead and Ollie Rattler, found her, half seated, half draped over the old hickory twig chair, only a dried husk of a human being, as brittle as the abandoned skeleton of an insect or the papery skin sloughed off by a rattlesnake. Dead, yes. There could be no doubt about that. For all practical purposes departed, but with no apparent inclination toward putrefaction now or any time. "She looked," Ira had said, "like somebody who died in a desert a hundred years ago."

"No stink neither," commented Ollie. "Whole place smelled like sulphured apples. A little musty. She must have put up a whole mess of them over the years, and you know how you can't never get the smell of dried apples out of nuthin'. Hell, do you remember Bob Pricey, Ira? Whew! Now that was a stink to make a dog...you know...revisit his vomit out of preference! "

I wish I were a lawyer and could write a fine hand,
I'd write to Miss Saro so she'd understand,
I'd write her by the river where the waters o'er flow,
And I'd think of Pretty Saro...wherever...I go.

Lucille bowed her head to indicate that she was through and stepped back from the grave. At that moment, a black crow dropped from the sky onto the twisted branch of a loblolly pine behind the mourners.

Peggie Whistle, the dwarf who ran the cash register for Dancing Chicken down in Saunooke Village, nudged Talahina in her ribs. "Late for her own funeral!" the dwarf whispered. The crow cocked its glossy head and peered closely at Peggie with a mica eye.

Josiah Etowah, the Baptist preacher from Yellow Hill, cast a nervous glance toward the crow and stepped tentatively forward. He cleared his throat cautiously. "Well, now, folks, I don't know rightly what I can say about this woman that we are burying here today," he began, with another uneasy glance in the crow's direction. "You know that we are all sinners in the eyes of the Lord...."

Who selected "Pretty Saro" as the song by which Mama Jesse would be laid in her grave, Talahina found herself wondering as Josiah rumbled on. He was trying valiantly to sidestep the issue of Mama Jesse's professional affiliation with what he, as a believing, which is not to say a good Baptist must of necessity see as the Powers of Darkness, but which most folks hereabouts reckoned were more properly considered the Powers of Nature—a dark and terrible Nature, to be sure, but Mother to us all. Talahina supposed that a wistful tale of a love not returned might have been an odd choice for a woman as full of years as Mama Jesse Black Crow had the old woman not spent a lifetime cauterizing with curses wounds of the heart.

"A sister may live far away from us, in a distant place," Josiah concluded his half-hearted eulogy. "She is still our sister. Bob Boxwell?"

He nodded to the funeral director from Bryson City, who, in turn, gave his two assistants the high sign. Slowly the ebony coffin, which was attached to a hoist, was slung into the open grave like cargo into the hold of a ship. Once the casket was firmly lodged in the grave and tamped down, the assistants disengaged the grappling hooks, packed away their gear and, together with Mr. Boxwell, jumped into their van and headed unceremoniously down the gravel road toward highway 19 and Bryson City.

"Sister Rollover," Josiah cued Lucille.

Lucille, whose daughter's life had been saved with Mama Jesse's help, knelt in a series of stages, like an elevator that sticks at each level—she was very fat and had an arthritic left hip that pained her—and gathered up a clump of red clap in her hands. She tossed it into the grave.

Then Molly, the daughter Mama Jesse had rescued, twenty

years old now but small still as a child, fell to her knees and Peggie, who might have been born a hedgehog had Mama Jesse not been on hand at her birth to ward away a lurking witch, and Talahina, who wished that she had known the witch of Rattlesnake Knob....

One by one the mourners joined Lucille and Molly and Peggie and Talahina in filling the old woman's grave with earth and building a high, smooth mound over it. Because grass does not grow well in clay, this mound, like the others in the New Burying Ground, would be raw and bare for decades to come. It is customary at Cherokee funerals for the mourners to fill in the grave with their own hands; this is the reason why no-one dresses up. Because the turnout for the funeral was so large (the conjure woman was famous; her charms and curses had shaped the histories of most of the families on the Boundary, which made her passing an event), the grave was filled in and the mound was built high and smoothed over in under a half an hour. Some children, caught up in the moment, continued to scoop up handfuls of mud long after the conjure woman lay safe and silent, unmoving, below a mound of clay that would bake in the summer sun to the colour of blood. As their parents and relatives visited, they threw the clumps at one another and laughed and yelled and ducked when the favour was returned and ran all over the burying ground like people who have gone temporarily insane.

Lucille, Peggie, Talahina and Molly sat on folding chairs, looking west from the Bald.

"I've got a joke for you," Peggie told Talahina. "Are you ready?" She always asked if her audience was ready, as if it was imperative to be braced. "Why do the Cherokee bury miscarried babies and white man don't?" she asked.

"I don't know," said Talahina.

"Because not too many Cherokee have flush toilets," said Peggie. "Hah! Hah!"

"Big Granny Tuskateeskee says that whatever has been in possession of a spirit, even for a short time, had best be put away for good," Lucille told her. "Otherwise it may wander around, causing trouble."

"Pah!" Peggie complained. "Spoken like an elder! Ghosts hanging from the rafters."

"So, what's going to happen with Mama Jesse's house?" Talahina asked Lucille. This is why she had come. The most important reason. She wanted Mama Jesse's house.

"I don't know," Lucille replied. "I don't think she had any legal title to the place, just squatter's rights. Her grandfather built it during the Removal. He was in hiding. An outlaw."

"I will live in it then," Talahina said.

"You're crazy, Talahina Bluebird!" Peggie exploded. "That cabin's haunted, and, even if it wasn't before, it will be now."

"I thought you didn't believe in ghosts," Talahina reminded her.

"Nobody in his right mind has gone near Rattlesnake Knob without a damned good reason for as long as anyone can remember," Peggie pointed out, "and now's no time to be starting!"

"I have to live somewhere," Talahina defended herself.

"You live with your Ma," Lucille reminded her.

"And my sister...and my brother-in-law...and their three children...and my other sister...and my brother," Talahina said. "There are so many vegetables in the stew that there is no room for the groundhog."

"What will you do all by yourself on top of that mountain at the end of that fireroad?" Molly asked.

"I was thinking I might learn to weave baskets," Talahina told her. "You know, the way they did in the old days."

"Weaving baskets is hard. Scarcely anybody around here knows how to do it anymore. Who do you think is going to teach you up there on Rattlesnake Knob?"Lucille asked.

"A ghost maybe," replied Talahina.

Talahina Bluebird was 25 years old the year she moved into Mama Jesse Black Crow's cabin on Rattlesnake Knob. She was a big woman, standing six feet, one and a half inches tall and weighing 193 pounds. Not fat so much as wide-hipped and broad shouldered, she occupied a great deal of space. Her appearence was arresting not merely because of her great size, but also because of her facial features. Her hawk nose, high, sloping cheekbones, prominent brows and heavy, square chin all seemed strangely overlarge, as if they had been hastily roughed out of a piece of wood and needed whittling and sanding down to bring them into a proper proportion—a doctor would have said that she suffered from a mild degree of giantism. The startling confluence of flaring planes and jutting promontories that was Talahina's face so dominated a casual observer's impression of her that, initially at least, her finer features often passed unnoticed. Those who knew her well, however, remarked upon the smooth copper radiance of her skin, the soft sheen of the long, straight black hair that she wore in two neat braids reaching to the middle of her back, the clearness and intelligence of her gold-flecked eyes, the suppleness of her mobile mouth and the graceful capability of her well made, big hands.

Talahina had a degree from UNC-Asheville in Anthropology. Most Cherokee with university degrees go on to teach at Cherokee schools—that is what a university degree is for—but Talahina did not want to teach school. Teaching school was too much doing, and that, according to Talahina, got in the way of any serious being. Since the age of thirteen, Talahina Bluebird had a secret ambition—she had confessed it to no-one. She wanted to be wise. Not knowledgeable. Wise. She wanted to be the wise old woman of the woods, to live on top of a high mountain and to give visitors seeking advice good counsel. She wanted to walk with the birds and the animals and feel one with them—she wanted to understand her animal nature. She wanted to have a notion of how reality was constructed, where the joins were. She wanted to know where dreams came from and what history really is. She was curious about time and she wanted to know if Indians were truly different from whites in any essential way and, if so, how. This was why, when the opportunity arose, she had commandeered Mama Jesse's cabin: it was high up, faraway; it was charged with a kind of energy—she could not describe or define or explain it, but she could feel it. So Talahina became a waitress at the Rocky Roadhouse and waited for something to occur to her.

She had been waitressing for four years when Ollie Rattler and Ira Bushyhead got on their CB and radioed in the news of Mama Jesse's death—Talahina picked the transmission up in her brother's pickup. That was when it occurred to her that she might take the conjure woman's place up in that remote cabin on Rattlesnake Mountain, and that notion, once formed, began to float in her mind like a dream that waking cannot dissolve.

In the second week of May, a fortnight after Mama Jesse's burial—she thought she'd give the conjure woman some time to settle—Talahina Bluebird took her brother's truck and drove up the fire road that cut through the pine forest mantling Rattlesnake Knob. Talahina had the use of her brother's truck until such time as he could pay her back for bailing him out of jail two years ago for sticking a white man. Talahina figured the truck was pretty much hers until the transmission fell out, seeing as Danny Bluebird was the shiftless, drinking sort, not likely to get a job any time soon and only this side of bars because nobody had been fool enough yet to make him mad enough to kill.

On her way to the cabin, she stopped for a few minutes by John and Sally Running Wolfs'to get some water for her radiator, which was leaking. The Running Wolves lived down mountain from Spiney Bole two miles and were to be her nearest neighbours. Folks had always credited this family with a kind of insane courage for biding so hard by Mama Jesse—it was generally agreed that conjure folk need plenty of room to expand and contract...like a bridge in a cold climate.

"You ever notice anything strange about the Black Crow place?" Talahina asked them.

"Oh, sometimes there'd be noises," Sally Running Wolf told her. "Sometimes sounded like a whole assembly of the Christian damned up there. Such moaning and screeching and weeping as you thought you'd never hear, no, not unless you were born at the time of the Second Coming."

John Running Wolf nodded. "We're used to it though," he said. "Lived here all our lives."

"Sometimes we'd be sitting in the front room and all of a sudden there's this glow and we look through the window and there's this ball of flame...oh, about as big as a baseball...and it's a-wafting slow like up the fire road toward Black Crow's," Sally told her. The woman nodded. "Mysterious-like," she concluded.

"We're safe here, though," John concluded. "Yup. Nothin's happened to us yet."

"Something sure got at those chickens, John," Sally contradicted him.

"It was a dog, Sally," John told her.

"Blood everywhere," Sally told Talahina. "A dog would have et 'em. Whatever this was just bloodied 'em. If I was you, I'd turn me right around and head me right back down mountain."

"Whyever, Sally?" asked John.

"Why, there's a headless chicken up there, John Running Wolf, and it's alive," Sally exclaimed. "I know because sometimes it wanders down here, and I have to shoo it away. Oh, it makes my blood run cold to see it stumbling around."

"Just don't know it's dead yet, Sally," John Running Wolf told his wife. He turned to Talahina. "A chicken's a stupid beast," he said. "My advice is just...you know...shoot it."

Talahina got back in the truck and headed up the mountain. The fire road was kept in pretty good nick by the government, but it was a dirt road just the same and her suspension was shot to hell, so she had to go slow. Just before she rounded the curve in the road that ended in the conjure woman's dooryard, a headless chicken staggered drunkenly into the road and stopped in the path of the truck. Talahina braked, and the truck lurched to a stop and then stalled. The chicken rallied itself slightly and, turning, picked its way through the ruts in the road to the forest at its edge. Tripping over the roots of a tree, it tumbled out of sight into the dark green of the quiet forest.

Talahina stood in the red clay dooryard, looking at Mama Jesse's cabin with some consternation. It had been hastily thrown up in the winter of 1838 to house renegade Black Crows fleeing white soldiers—had the white soldiers been able to locate the Black Crows, they would have crowded them into the stockade at Ross' landing and marched them to the Oklahoma territory along with 18,000 of their tribesmen. The cabin had been built to suffice a season. After 160 winters, it resembled nothing so much as a woodpile of deadfall from which a ramshackle, falling down porch haphazardly protruded.

Talahina stepped onto the porch. Two gnarled twig rockers the bleached colour of driftwood rocked creakily on the porch, set off by a faint breeze that ran through the boughs of the trees surrounding the dooryard like fingers brushing softly and repetitively the strings of a Jew's harp. The floorboards shrieked under her tread like old knees cracking. She bent to look more closely at one of the rockers. A green shoot sprang from the seemingly dead wood. At its tip was a tender, tightly furled leaf. She was reaching out to touch it, when a dog's head suddenly hove into view from behind the far side of the porch and dull eyes, filmed bluely with cataracts, peered questioningly at her.

"Hello, dog," said Talahina. She was not scared of dogs.

The loose skin on top of the dog's head swam together, hiking up two chewed ears. With some difficulty the animal managed to haul his hind quarters off the ground. Balancing unsteadily on his four feet, he lumbered awkwardly onto the porch, his frantically wagging tail wreaking such havoc with his equilibrium that he listed dangerously to one side. He was a mangy bag of bones kind of dog, about a hundred years old.

Talahina patted him on the head. "I'll call you Jake on account of the country song, If I die before I wake…feed Jake," she told the dog, which promptly keeled over and lay on his side, panting ecstatically, his ribs heaving. She scratched him under the chin. "I'll buy you a flea collar," she promised by way of cementing the relationship, then, straightening up, she stepped over Jake and, taking the door by its wooden handle, pushed it open and peered inside.

The cabin was dimly lit by means of two small windows. Both of these were covered in oilcloth, which had darkened with age and soot from the woodstove. After the moment needed for Talahina's eyes to adjust to the gloom, she took a deep breath and stepped inside, leaving the door ajar—the musty scent of dried apples emanating from the cabin's interior was strong enough to be a little heady. Jake reassembled himself and lurched after her.

The cabin's interior consisted of one room about ten feet square and a leanto about six feet long and six feet deep. The leanto could be separated from the main room by drawing across the opening the faded Star of Bethlehem quilt—what mountain folk call a kiverlid—suspended by bone rings from a wooden dowel pegged into the leanto's side walls. The leanto contained a narrow cot, over which a blue and white Road to Dover quilt was thrown, and an old pine dresser. Talahina squeezed the flat pillow and checked under the quilt: both mattress and pillow were feather ticking, soft and scratchy and smelling faintly of the barnyard.

The main room was similar to other back country cabins with which she was familiar: the floor was bright yellow poplar, with boards three feet wide and from the darkened beams hung dried herbs and strings of field corn and red and yellow peppers. However, the walls of both the main room and the leanto were papered closely with faded sheets from old newspapers instead of the more typical coat of whitewash. Talahina moved along one wall, peering closely in the dim light to read headlines. Among excerpts from the more recent Cherokee One Feathers were bits and pieces from the *Cherokee Phoenix*, the newspaper printed in Cherokee and put out by Elias Boudinot prior to the 1838 Removal—copies of the *Phoenix* were exceedingly rare. The walls had been sealed with several coats of shellac. They glowed dully yellow in the half light.

She looked up.

At one end of the main room an old woodstove skulked. Another old twig rocker, like those creaking away on the porch outside, was drawn close to the stove, a grey woven shawl draped neatly over one gnarled, knotty arm—presumably it was in this chair, Talahina reflected, that the Cherokee police had found the strangely dessicated body of Mama Jesse Black Crow.

A roughly hewn table stood in the centre of the room on which were set half a dozen thick pottery cups of a dull green colour, a battered copper bowl filled with withered apples and a tool with which she was not familiar. It consisted of a long metal blade with a handle attached at a right angle on one end, presumably for leverage. Like the rocker outside, she could make out several points at which the table had sprouted tender, living shoots. It was as if it were somehow still living, its four legs trunks leading to subterranean roots.

The end of the room opposite the woodstove was taken up with a large, rambling pine cupboard. Moving over to it, Talahina opened one of its several doors, then another. The cupboard was shallow, no more than a handspan deep, and equipped with narrow shelves on which were jars neatly labelled in a careful spidery hand: mistletoe and love-all-in-a-tangle, ground jimsonweed burrs, gill-go-by-the-ground, bethany. Talahina pawed through the jars. Water pressed from the lung of a sheep from which the blood has been allowed to drain, she read on the back of one flask. Beside it stood a beaker of walnut water: water from a walnut tree in which an incision has been made. "Listen to this," she told Jake the dog. "Splinters from a tree struck by lightning; pastes of earthworm; cobwebs...." but Jake, exhausted by enthusiasm, just lay panting on his side. Talahina pulled open one of the drawers in the cupboard. There, on loose pieces of paper, yellowed with age, were notes, penned in the same careful schoolbook hand, "Cure dropsy with three scruples of loadstone powder taken with fennel juice," she read. "What is dropsy?" she asked Jake. He didn't know. "Treat burns with a plaster of tar.... What are these beads for? And these shells?" The cupboard was clearly Mama Jesse's pharmacy. Her assistance had been sought in cases where a curse might be considered overkill after all—persistent coughs, for example, or sore nipples.

"I'll start here," Talahina announced to the dog. "I will put all of this stuff in some kind of order." So saying, she took all the contents of the cupboard out and placed them on the table. Then she opened each jar and flask and smelled it to see if anything had gone moldy or off—a few had; these she threw out. Next she wiped the jars and flasks with a damp cloth, and replaced them on the shelves, this time in strictly alphabetical order: agrimony, alum-root, angelica, anise...wormwood, yarrow, yaupon. It took her well over two hours. In the end, she counted 102 receptacles. Then she set about sorting the beads from the shells and the feathers from the stones and the teeth and the claws.

Finally she dumped all of the scraps of paper on which Rowena had scrawled recipes and formulas into the shoebox her Hush Puppies had come in. "There's no sorting these now," she told Jake. "That's going to take a long time." She would tuck the box under the bed for the time being, she decided. Then she could browse through them at her leisure . She crossed to the cot, dropped down on her knees, lifted the

Road to Dover quilt and was on the point of tucking the box under the cot when she discovered the wooden box wrapped in an ancient and almost papery piece of buckskin.

Gingerly she removed it from under the bed, stood and walked to the table. She set it on the table, opened it and, bending over, peered inside. At its bottom lay an oblong object about two or three inches long and wrapped in a smaller piece of deerskin. Tentatively she took hold of the deerskin, lifted the packet out of the pot and gave it a light shake. In that same instant she was dazzled by a sudden flash of light, the cold white green colour sheet lightning is. She dropped back a step, turning her head and shielding her eyes. Then she blinked and looked back again. There, lying before her on the rough table, was a triangular crystal, flat on the bottom with slightly convex sides tapering up to a point. The crystal was perfectly transparent except for a single red streak running through it from top to bottom, and it was pulsating unevenly with the same cold light which had flashed so blindingly at her a moment before.

"Law!" exclaimed Talahina softly. "It's not. It is." She backed away from the table, her hand at her throat. She might not have come from a family that kept the old ways—the Bluebirds played Bingo for profit and bowled in leagues—but even the Bluebirds would have known what the object on Mama Jesse's sprouting table was. "An ulunsuti!" Talahina murmurered to herself incredulously. "Goddam!"

Ulunsutis conferrred upon their owners success in all things—in hunting, in love, in rainmaking, but particularly in prophecy. When an ulunsuti was consulted for the purpose of ascertaining future events, it mirrors what is to pass the same way a quiet stream reflects the image of a tree standing on its bank—it reflects recovery from illness, return from battle, old age achieved.... Images that lie folded in the arms of the future.

"Oh, shit," Talahina exclaimed. "The last thing I need! A magic eight ball!"

The down side to owning an ulunsuti is that every seven days it must be rubbed with the blood of a recent kill and twice a year at least with the blood of a deer or other large animal. Should its owner not feed it at the proper time, it emerges from its hiding place at night in the shape of a ball of fire and flies through the air to slake its thirst with somebody's lifeblood. Guess I know who's been at the Running Wolfs' chickens, she thought.

At that moment the headless chicken lurched through the door and stood reeling before the table—it was plain that it was collecting itself. After a few moments, it carefully negotiated a turn and tottered unsteadily back out the door.

"That chicken is getting on my nerves," Talahina commented.

Talahina was asleep and dreaming in Mama Jesse Black Crow's cabin. In her dream, the curtain separating the lean-to from the main room of Rowena's cabin was pulled open. This was odd because Talahina had drawn it when she had gone to sleep that night—the cabin faced east and grew almost painfully bright in the early morning; it lit up with a white dusty radiance that had something otherworldly about it, as if it emanated from a spaceship hovering over Rattlesnake Knob. Seated at the sprouting table but turned toward Talahina was a tall, angular woman wearing a long, dark shirtwaist dress and a rather battered bonnet. Like Talahina, she seemed overlarge but lacked the waitress' essential bulk. Hers was a loose concatenation of big, knobby bones. In the darkened room, she seemed very pale to Talahina. Over time, the dead tend to fade.

After a moment in which she composed her thoughts, Talahina asked, "Who are you?"

"Sophia Sawyer," the woman replied.

"Where do you come from?" Talahina wanted to know.

"Oh, I am hung up here," Sophia told her both matter-of-factly and wistfully. "It's like when you snag your skirt on a rosebush and you pull and pull but can't break free, not without tearing something."

"I see," said Talahina.

"That's how it is," said Sophia.

The two women fell silent. After a moment, Talahina observed, "I'm dreaming, I think."

"I'm afraid not," Sophia told her.

"I'm dead?"

"No, I'm dead," Sophia corrected her. "You're visiting me. Often as not, what people call dreams are actually visits with the dead."

"But I dream every night," said Talahina.

"No, actually you visit the dead every night," Sophia said.

"I wouldn't forget a thing like that...like a visit with a dead person," Talahina protested.

"Of course you would. You do. You do all the time. You'll forget this visit upon waking," Sophia predicted.

"I won't!" cried Talahina.

"Mark my words," said Sophia.

Silence once again. Sophia sighed and shifted in her chair. She seemed listless. "No needlework," she complained. "Nothing passes the time like it."

"When did you die?" asked Talahina, by way of conversation.

Sophia shrugged. "I've ceased to measure time. What's the point?"

"I'm not dead yet," Talahina reminded her. "For me there's still a point. I want to know when you lived. You look sort of like one of those pioneer women to me."

"I remember the date 1824," Sophia offered.

"Was that when you were born?" Talahina asked.

Sophia shook her head. "Not when I was born.... When I began to live. I came south from New Hampshire to teach at the Brainerd Academy in 1824."

"That Baptist mission school over in Tennessee?" Talahina asked.

"Yes," said Sophia. "I was so happy there. Ecstatic. I was not happy in New Hampshire."

"Why not?" asked Talahina.

"Mine is a passionate nature," Sophia explained. "I was not understood." She shrugged. "I taught little children. Many of them could not speak English. I went with them to the swimming hole and organized berry-picking parties and took them on picnics to places where the larks made nests or deer were apt to come. I explained what makes a cricket chirp and taught them to see extraordinary things in the stars. They taught me...how to be."

Talahina raised herself to her elbows. "They knew how to be?" she asked.

"Back then, they did," Sophia replied. "But the Cherokees were so eager to become like white men.... No other Indian tribe adopted the ways of the white man to the same extent that the Cherokee did. They were remarkable for that. By the time I arrived in Tennessee, the chiefs owned plantations that were worked by black men. They drove fine carriages and wore white man's clothes. Peacocks strutted in the front yards of their big houses. They established a government on the federal model, omitting a treasury—this proved to be a great mistake when they later needed money. They raised money through speaking tours of all civilized things for a printing press and published a newspaper...."

"The Phoenix," said Talahina, glancing around at her walls.

"The poorer Cherokee was truer to his ancestors than the rich chiefs," continued Sophia. "Still he emulated the clothes of his white neighbour...and the way he built his house and sowed his crops. The cruel surprise came when the Cherokee discovered that, civilized or no, the presence of Indians in these mountains was simply not going to be tolerated by the white man, that the Cherokee had become like the white man in order to be accepted by him but that it had, in the long run, made absolutely no difference. That was a hard lesson, and, in the learning of it, many of them forgot what it was to be

Indian." She paused. "There was also a lot of death," she added, shaking her head. "So many on the trail. It made everybody a little crazy."

"The Cherokee have been a nation in shock for more than a century," agreed Talahina.

"Shock can be fatal," said Sophia.

Talahina nodded her head slowly. "Yes," she agreed. "You are right. But I am tired. I am going to go to sleep now."

Sophia smiled wanly and stood. Standing, she resembled a beam of light. "See you tomorrow night," she said.

Knowledge spreads like a slow stain, colouring what is permeable. That night Talahina dreamed of a white oak tree, tall and straight. She thought from the way in which the tree cast its shadow that it must grow on the north side of a mountain. She dreamed many other things, but this she remembered.

The following night, Sophia Sawyer introduced the waitress to an Indian woman. "This is Lottie Stamper," she told her.

Lottie stood about four feet ten and was plumply soft, with dimpled elbows and a double chin riding on a roll of fat. Her iron grey hair was pulled back from her pleasant, almost pretty face in a loose braid. She was just the least bit transparent. The first thing she did was to pick up the strange cutting tool that Talahina had seen lying on the table.

"Good," she said . "You have a froe already." The word as Lottie pronounced it rhymed with throw. "Now you need a saw."

"What for?" asked Talahina.

"To cut down that white oak on the north side of the mountain," Lottie told her matter-of-factly. "You'll also need a wedge and a glut and a mallet. For a wedge, you can use the crotch of a large, fallen tree if you have one, but the glut should be cut out of hardwood—dogwood or persimmon or ironwood beech are good."

"Wait a minute! Wait a minute!" Talahina protested. "Why do I need all those things?"

"To rive your pole," answered Lottie. "You do want to make baskets, don't you?"

During the first year that Talahina lived at Mama Jesse Black Crow's cabin she learned how to doubleweave baskets.

She learned that white oak was the preferred wood of basketmakers, but that hickory, maple, white or black ash were also good.

She discovered that hickory, which is slightly more dense than oak and very springy, makes excellent handles and rims but is more difficult to split into thin strips than oak, and that the perfect white oak is nearly always found growing in mature forests on the north side of mountain slopes.

She learned how to work with honeysuckle and blackberry canes and one-year shoots of dogwood and sassafras. She hunted river cane and mulberry and red maple either early in the year—before the snakes awake in the woods—or in autumn, when the vines are longest.

She split willow the way Indians do—using her teeth and both hands—and soaked the tree trunks she chose, pounding the bark until single splints could be stripped free of the pole.

Her collection of tools grew. In addition to a wedge and a glut and a mallet and a froe, she acquired an awl made from the rear leg bone of an old horse and a cow's horn for coiling straw as well as pruning-shears for cutting green vines and a sickle for harvesting the pale gold bearded winter wheat or oatstraw that she bound with the red-mahoghany bark of raspberry canes or hung, bound in bundles around the seed heads, from the beams of Mama Jesse's cabin.

Talahina learned how to weave a slew and a french slew and a wale and a randing. She chased with two colours. She became expert at the pairing weave but did it the way Indians do, with the top weaver twisted counter rather than clockwise.

She collected roots and leaves to make her own dyes and used the dead woman's big copper kettle to dye her light colours and Mama Jesse's iron pot for darker hues: sassafras for a soft yellow tan, indigo for blue, madder for scarlet, cochineal for rose.

She filled a five gallon paint can with walnuts and set the can in the open to collect rainwater and steep throughout the winter, straining off the saturated dark brown dye into plastic milk jugs every two months or so.

She learned that the steeped bark of white oak from a clay soil containing a high percentage of alum, like that over toward Alum Cave Bluffs, gave off a bronze-grey colour while trees bastard-cut from around Rattlesnake Knob yielded a purple-silver grey hue and that both colours were beautiful in their own right.

She discovered that, although spring-cut willow is white, processing the withes releases the tannin in the bark, staining the splints a buff tan colour.

She found out that any wood to be dyed in a water bath must first be trimmed and smoothly planed, even sanded, before it is soaked—water raises the wood's grain, giving the basket a coarse look—and that the only finishing a basket needs is oil from the human hand, applied over years of use. Anything else, a linseed oil finish or a varnish, does not allow the pores of the thin wood to contract and expand with changes of humidity and attracts dust and grime.

She burned cedar bark and used the ashes as a mordant. She also used alum and vinegar or sometimes rusty nails, depending on the colour. She collected her urine over the course of a few days and set it in the sun. She found that this set her dyes very well.

Down at the Qualla Coop the manager Bob Bobwhite commented that Talahina's baskets were among the finest he had ever seen. "Who taught you to make baskets this way?" he asked. "There are only a few Cherokee women alive who can make baskets this good."

"The ghosts of our ancestors," Talahina replied and laughed, so Bob Bobwhite knew that he was not to take her too seriously.

He did take her seriously though. "They are good teachers," he told her.

"I have a joke," Peggie Whistle told Talahina.

"I am not surprised," said Talahina. The two women were seated at Talahina's table, drinking tea.

"The following are questions on the Civil Service Exam," explained Peggie. "This is the test that white people take so that they can work at the Bureau of Indian Affairs. Are you ready?"

"Yes," said Talahina.

"What is a silver dollar mostly made of?" asked Peggie.

"Silver," said Talahina.

"Here's another," said Peggie, warming up. "Can you explain Einstein's theory? Yes or no?"

Talahina laughed.

"Wait!" cried Peggie. "This is one of my favourites. A man builds a house with four sides to it. You know, it's rectangular in shape. Each side has a southern exposure. A big bear wanders by. What is the colour of the bear?"

"That question doesn't make any sense," complained Talahina.

"That's why it's funny!" exclaimed Peggie, wheezing with excitement; she was on a roll. "What about this: a woman gives a beggar 50¢. The woman is the beggar's sister. The beggar is not the woman's brother. Who is this person?"

"Peggie!" Talahina protested.

"What's in this tea?" Peggie asked.

"Jimsonweed burrs," said Talahina. "Ground."

"Tastes like an old Christmas tree," said Peggie. "White men owe a lot to the Indians. Do you know that? Who mined all the gold and silver that made Europe so rich? And what about potatoes?"

"Or chocolate," added Talahina.

"Or peppers," asked Peggie.

"What about quinine?" said Talahina.

"Caucus is an Indian word," said Peggie. "I don't know quite what it means though." Absently she fingered one of the green shoots sent forth from the table. "This table is alive," she commented. She roused herself. "Now," she said. "What is it I do here?"

Talahina took from her the hen basket she was teaching the dwarf to weave—increasingly over the past year women had begun to come to her so that they might learn her art; the waitress had become a teacher. Peggie was weaving her basket from hickory splints stained red-orange from bloodroot and set with a mordant made from rusty nails. "You tighten the weaver until the centre rises to a slight peak," Talahina explained carefully. "See? The notches make it easy. Here, let me show you. Like this."

A black crow sat on a branch outside Talahina's window. Through the yellowed oilcloth she noted the bird's familiar stark and upright shape. Talahina realized that the crow knew who the beggar in Peggie Whistle's joke really was...that, and many other things as well. She understood that it knew things the way a bird knows them—not with words, but with images strung on lines of feeling, blown by the faint breeze that travels these coves and hills like an itinerant messenger come all the way from the home of lightning and the resting place of the wind, from that secret mountain place where what was and what will be shadow dance around a constant fire .

Epilogue: Constant Fire

One evening long ago, during the second intermission of "Unto These Hills," a little white boy extinguished the eternal flame located at the top of the theatre in a stone grotto. He peed on it. A plaque bolted to the rocks of the grotto tells the story of the flame: it had been kindled from the sacred fire taken west by the Cherokee to the Oklahoma territory.

The flame was quickly reignited, and a lucite shield was installed over it to protect it in the future. On the whole, the Cherokee in the drama were more sanguine about the incident than I would have thought likely. "White men," they said,

147

shrugging. "They pee on everything." Far more important than the eternal flame, I was assured by the old women, was the constant fire of the Cherokee.

In the old days, the constant fire was that which was kindled at the time a village was built. This is how it worked. At the centre of the village was its townhouse, and the townhouse was built upon a mound. When the people were ready to build the mound, they laid a circle of stones on the surface of the ground and made a fire in its centre. Near the fire they placed the body of some important chief or priest who had recently died, together with a Ulunsuti, an Uktena scale or horn, the feather from the right wing of an eagle or a great hawk and beads of seven colours—red, white, black, blue, purple, yellow and grey. The priest then conjured these with disease so that, if an enemy should ever invade and destroy the townhouse, he would die and never return to his people.

The Cherokee set a long, hollow cedar trunk, with the bark still on, carefully over the fire. Then the women brought earth in baskets and built up the mound, piling dirt above the stones, the bodies of their great men and sacred things but never above the end of the hollow log. That always remained free of earth so that the fire below might be fed on oxygen. From this fire all the fires in the village were lit.

The last constant fire recorded in existence had been in Kituhwa. Kituhwa, which means The Middle, is a mound about three miles northeast of Bryson City on U.S. 19. The settlement there had been an important one. It had given its name to one of the Cherokee dialects and, upon occasion, to the tribe as a whole: Ani Kituhwa, "People of Kituhwa." Cherokee soldiers reported seeing smoke from the mound at the time of the Civil War, I was told.

One day, I went out to Kituhwa to see if, by any chance, the flame still burned. The mound lies in a field on the south side of the highway a short distance behind a converted airplane hangar. The field has been cultivated for generations; corn leaches the earth of its ancient memories. I looked all around the spot. There was no sign of smoke. Then a storm broke out; the Thunder Boys spoke to me from the Darkening Land and the sky turned black and rain roared around me like a waterfall. I drove back to Cherokee and told the old women that there was no more constant fire.

"Of course there is a constant fire," they told me. "It is hidden."

"Where?" I asked.

They looked at each other and tipped backwards in their rocking-chairs. They were making beaded belts and held needles to the light to thread them, squinting old eyes. Jars of glass beads sat open at their feet and strips of leather lay across their laps. "Ha!" They laughed laughs as short as barks. "Ha!"

"A smart hiding place," said one.

"No-one will ever find it," agreed another.

A third motioned me closer. "Pst," she said.

"What?" I asked, leaning forward.

"Did you never wonder why these mountains are called the Smokies?" she asked.